SHORT STORIES FOR RAINY DAYS

Short Stories for Rainy Days

M. E. Keimig

iUniverse, Inc.
New York Lincoln Shanghai

Short Stories for Rainy Days

iUniverse, Inc.

For information address:
iUniverse, Inc.
2021 Pine Lake Road, Suite 100
Lincoln, NE 68512
www.iuniverse.com

ISBN: 0-595-33596-9

Printed in the United States of America

CONTENTS

▼

MIRAGE

The cell phone rang and Jack Landon reached over to turn off the "U2" CD he began listening to when he got into the car and started on his way to Las Vegas. Strains of "Beautiful Day" faded off as he hit the pause button and reached for the phone. Remembering that he set it into the hands free speaker mode, he pushes the answer button, returning his hand to the sleek leather covered steering wheel.

"It's your dime, speak to me."

"Phone calls haven't been a dime in my lifetime Jack. You're dating yourself again. What's your ETA back to Vegas? We've got some presentations to go over before you meet with Mr. Raphael at his new hotel tomorrow."

Jack sped up to pass a maroon Pontiac Grand Prix in front of him. Droplets of rain pelted his windshield. "The traffic hasn't been too bad from Salt Lake City, so I'm making good time. I should only be about three hours out. It's starting to rain, but that shouldn't slow me down too much. Just keep the coffee hot and I'll be there before you know it."

He could hear his secretary's sigh of disgust over the phone.

"I don't know why you just can't fly like everyone else, Jack. It would be a lot faster than all these road trips you make. I know you don't like flying, but there are more accidents on the road than there are up in the sky."

Jack smiled as he reached over to turn his CD back on.

But I love driving. My life doesn't depend on whether some pilot is having a good day or not. I have my own control panel in my BMW Z8 and I'm doing my own flying here on Earth. Talk to ya later, Sheila."

The rain droplets turned into a downpour, making visibility crappy even with the windshield wipers going at top speed. He followed along Interstate 15 for another twenty miles when he noticed orange cones and arrow signs pointing to the right. Traffic was being directed to one lane and then detoured onto a county road. Road construction season had already begun. Jack's good mood had been dampened by more than just the rain as he muttered under his breath.

"Oh for…geez. I can't believe this. Looks like the coffee's gonna get cold, Sheila. It'll be at least another two hours with these damn detours." Jack pulled off the interstate and followed the detour signs for the next forty miles, hoping to find his way back onto the main road again. The rain continued to fall at a heavy pace and traffic was slowing down. Frustration setting in, Jack decided he had enough of following the car in front of him and moved closer to get ready to pass. As he neared the blue Ford Taurus, he read the personalized plate, "Xanadu," before moving into the next lane. He didn't have much time to get back into the right lane since the oncoming traffic was closer than he thought. He quickly pulled back in, the blue Ford behind him now. "Xanadu," geez. Why don't you drive in Xanadu with the other slow-pokes and stay off the highways."

Just then, Jack heard a loud noise. Thinking it was thunder, he looked up through his windshield, but couldn't see any lightning. He shrugged and continued following along the detour. He drove for another half hour when he realized that the rain had stopped.

The afternoon sun blared down on his red BMW and he hit the switch that powered his convertible top. He felt like his old self again, driving with the top down, a warm breeze ruffling his sandy hair that had just enough gray on the temples to make him look distinguished, an affect for which he paid his hairdresser dearly.

He punched some buttons on his dashboard, trying to access the navigational system that was programmed in his car. The screen remained blank. He pushed the speed dial for his office on his cell phone, but it displayed 'out of service'. "Damn. These high tech doo-dads are great unless you're out in the middle of nowhere, and that's when you really need them!"

He couldn't find any highway signs to tell him where he was or what road he was on. He'd made the trip from Salt Lake City to Las Vegas often, but none of what he was seeing looked familiar. The pleasant scenery that he usually enjoyed when he drove this way was now flat, sandy desert. He would drive past lakes and trees and towering red clay rock formations. There wasn't anything like that for miles that he could see. He was definitely lost. He parked along the shoulder and pulled out a map from his glove box. Looking around, he could see no other cars passing this way. Where was the blue Ford he passed, that was right behind him?

He unfolded the map, but not knowing what road he was on made it difficult to figure out where he was. He traced his finger along the road he exited on to from the interstate. "I can't be that far off the beaten path. How the hell did I wind up in the desert?" He looked at his gas gauge as he refolded his map. "Half a tank still, oh well, that should hopefully get me to civilization somewhere down this road."

He started up the car and drove back onto the highway, but before he got up to speed he noticed a girl sitting on the side of the road. She looked liked she was in her early twenties, with long auburn hair that seemed like a wild fire blazing in the hot afternoon sun. She appeared to be sitting there, leaning against a gray knap sack, staring out at the highway as if she were waiting for someone or something. Always one for a pretty face, Jack slowed down once again and parked on the shoulder a few feet from where she sat.

As he got out of his car, she looked up at him but still remained seated, her legs folded behind her, mostly covered by the long green cotton dress that she wore. He noticed she was barefoot when he got close enough to talk to her. "Kind of a strange place to be waiting for a ride, out here in the middle of nowhere. I don't think much traffic comes this way. I wouldn't be here myself, if it wasn't for getting lost after being detoured off the main road. Need a lift?"

Her eyes took his breath away and words escaped him, something Jack never had a problem with ever before. They were turquoise, blue like the ocean he surfed in Maui last year. He could drown in those eyes. He was already having trouble coming up for air. He reached his hand down to help her up from the ground. She looked at it for a second and then brought her own hand up to his and let him help her up.

"Excuse the cliché, but what's a nice girl like you doing out here in a place like this?" He held the passenger car door open for her as she got in, placing her knap sack by her feet in the front seat. He closed the door and walked around the car and got back behind the steering wheel. He placed the key into the ignition, but waited before turning it, looking at his passenger inquiringly. She pulled the seat belt over her and clicked it into place and then looked up at him with a hint of a smile playing on her lips.

"The car I was in became incapacitated, leaving me without transportation. I was able to walk a few miles before it got too hot to go any further. That is where you just found me. I appreciate the ride. You can just drop me off at the nearest town." Her words seemed lofty and stilted to Jack. Who used the word 'incapacitated'? There were better words that Jack could think of to use when his car stalled on him. Oh well, it didn't matter. She was still a sight for sore eyes. At least she improved the scenery.

"Sure, no problem. I need to stop at the next town for gas anyway. You can probably make arrangements for a tow at the station we stop at. So, where were you headed for before your car broke down? If you were on your way to Vegas, I could take you all the way. I'm going there anyway." She looked out the window as she shook her head slightly. "I'm not really sure where I'm going yet, but thanks for the offer."

Now it was Jack's turn to shake his head as he thought to himself. "She's a looker, but I don't think there's too much going on up there in that pretty head of hers. Maybe she sat in the sun too long or something." He started the car and drove back onto the road. "By the way, my name's Jack. May I ask you yours? It makes for nice company if one knows the other's name. Saves me from having to address you as 'Miss,' or would it be 'Ma'am'? She turned around and looked at him, her eyes seeming to reach deep into his soul; that's if he still had one. A life of wheeling and dealing in Vegas makes one forget sometimes. "It's Miss; I am not married. My name is Kalyca."

Jack's speedometer read 80 as he set his cruise control on the convertible. The wind became stronger as he sped up and caused the auburn hair to billow around her shoulders. He would've liked to touch that hair, but he didn't want to frighten her. There were too many nuts out there that made it unsafe for women to accept a ride from. He didn't want her to think he was one of them. "That's an unusual name, kind of pretty. Does it mean anything?"

She reached into her knap sack and pulled out a paisley scarf that she tied around her hair to keep it from flying. "It means 'rosebud'. My mother loved words; she was an English professor. She also loved flowers and kept a beautiful garden. When she chose my name she looked up many words that translated into names of flowers and when she came upon Kalyca, she knew it was the one that she would bestow on me. She decorated my nursery with rosebuds of all different colors on the walls and the bedding, and planted a rose bush on the day I was born."

Jack noticed that her face lit up and she smiled as she spoke of her mother. "You speak of her in the past tense. I guess she's no longer around, huh?"

Kalyca's smile faded as she gently shook her head. "No, she's no longer around, but I am still always with her."

Jack stopped talking for awhile, a first for him, as they continued down the highway. He didn't think she was interested in conversation anyway but the companionship on this lonely roadway was enough for now. After driving for another hour, they finally came upon a town. "Looks like we made it none too soon. The tank was getting low there and I didn't fancy having to walk that hot stretch like you did." The sign read 'Welcome to Egarim" as he took the car out of cruise control and slowed down, following the main street to a gas station on his left.

As he drove into the station, steam started coming out from under the hood. A man, who looked to be in his thirties and was wearing coveralls, came out just as Jack was opening up the hood. "Would you like me to take a look at that, mister?" Jack swore when his hand touched something hot as he perused under the hood. "This is turning out to be one long and shitty day. Yeah, could you take a look? It appears driving through the desert doesn't agree with my $130,000.00 car."

Jack moved aside as the man leaned over and, using a rag, reached in and looked over the engine, checking the oil and the radiator hose. "I guess it doesn't matter how much your car is worth when it's not working. Looks like you got a hole in your radiator hose. I'm not sure if we have one that would fit your car, but I'll go and check." Jack turned as he heard his car door open and saw Kalyca reaching over for her bag as she was getting out of the vehicle. "Thank you for the ride, Jack. I can make it from here." For some reason that he couldn't explain, he didn't want her to leave. He felt this over powering need to protect her, from what, he didn't know.

Jack looked around and noticed a restaurant just across the road. "Hey, why don't you let me buy you some lunch? It looks like I'm going to be here for awhile and it's going to take them some time to get your vehicle towed in and find out what's wrong with it, after they fix mine that is." The man walked back out from the garage and came over to Jack.

"Looks like you lucked out. I just happen to have the right hose. It'll take about an hour before its ready. I'm just finishing up another car, and then I'll get right on it." Jack told him about Kalyca's car and made arrangements for him to tow it in when he could and work on it. "We'll be over at the restaurant. Fill it up with gas, too, when you're done."

Jack reached over and pulled out his cell phone before taking Kalyca's arm and gently pulling her across the street. "Come on, you see that it's going to take awhile. You may as well be comfortable." Kalyca looked resigned as she allowed Jack to take her arm.

He tried his cell phone again, but it was still dead. "Sheila's going to kill me when I don't show up this afternoon." Kalyca waited as Jack reached out to open the door of the restaurant for her. "Who's Sheila?" Jack followed behind her into the air-conditioned building, which felt like heaven to him after being out in the 100 degree heat. "She's my secretary, but sometimes I swear she's bossier than I am."

The restaurant had the usual southwestern motif, with desert murals on the walls and fake cacti positioned purposely around the room to add to the affect. They were led to a table by the front window where they could look out at the gas station. "Well, it's not the best view, but at least I'll be able to see when they finish with my car."

The waitress came over with menus and two glasses of water, placing them on the table between them. Jack glanced around the room. There were only three other couples, which didn't bother him at all. He hated crowds. They both ordered iced teas. Jack would've preferred a cold beer, but he knew that he still had a long drive ahead of him. As they waited for their sandwiches to arrive, he tried to find out more about this mysterious woman seated across from him.

"So, have you figured out where you're going yet?" She didn't seem to hear his question, her attention focused on something else behind him. He turned to see what she was looking at. It was a mural of a garden with exotic trees and flowers. It didn't quite fit in with the desert theme, but he found it sort of peaceful to look at. He turned back to Kalyca as she continued to stare at the wall. "…And there were gardens bright with sinuous rills where blossomed many an incense-bearing tree; And here were forests ancient as the hills, enfolding sunny spots of greenery." She turned her eyes toward him again, a light blush rising on her cheeks. "It's one of my favorites." Jack looked puzzled as he watched her while the waitress came with their meals.

After the waitress left again he leaned over to Kalyca. "What is one of your favorites?"

She put down the sandwich she was about to bite into and nodded toward the wall. "The mural reminded me of a favorite poem of mine, 'Xanadu', by Coleridge. My mother recited it for me when I was a little girl." She picked up her sandwich again and began eating it. Jack washed down the first half of his sandwich with a long draught of iced tea, an inkling of a memory stirring in his brain. "Xanadu, I know I've come across that word recently." He looked out the window and spotted the tow truck from the gas station bringing in a vehicle. Dangling loosely off the back bumper was a license plate that triggered his memory. "That's it! I passed a car today on the road that had a license plate 'Xanadu' on it. Actually, it was that car. That's a weird coincidence…I mean…" Jack paused, looking at Kalyca and then back at the car now parked outside the gas station.

"Hey, it's your car isn't it? Wow, that is some coincidence; I may have to read that poem someday."

Kalyca smiled at Jack as she placed her napkin on her empty plate and stood up. "There are no coincidences, Jack. Just like there are no accidents, either." Jack got up too, and placed a twenty dollar bill on the table. "Then what do you call it when you see two or more vehicles out on the road collide into one another?" Kalyca stepped outside as Jack held the door for her. "I call it someone out on the road being stupid." Jack shrugged as he walked with her back to the gas station. "I guess you can't argue with that. I've met some of those stupid drivers."

Jack walked over to where he found his BMW parked. The mechanic had been standing over by the car he had just towed in, but walked over to Jack when he saw him. "It's all fixed up with a full tank of gas." He handed Jack the bill. "Do you take credit cards?" The mechanic nodded as Jack pulled his Visa out of his wallet and placed it in his hand. While he waited for the mechanic to process the card, he walked over to the car that had just been detached from the tow hook. He noticed the front end was all crushed in and the driver's door was dented. Glass lay on the seat from the broken windshield. He leaned his head in and looked closer at the front seat. The driver's seat was stained with blood. He looked up at Kalyca who watched him from the other side of the vehicle. "This can't be your car. If you were driving this you would have been seriously hurt. There's not a scratch on you!"

The mechanic heard Jack as he came up behind him. "No, she wasn't driving this vehicle. Hers must still be out there. We'll drive out and look for it again later." Jack turned around and took the receipt that the mechanic handed him after signing his name on the slip. "Why are you so certain that she wasn't driving this vehicle? I mean I know it looks impossible, but stranger things have happened. Sometimes there's a lot of blood and only minor cuts and bruises." The mechanic gave him back his card and leaned against the car. "I came upon the accident while looking for the lady's vehicle, thinking this was it. The sheriff asked me to tow the vehicle off the road for them since I was there anyway. He said that from what he could make out from the tire marks, it looked like someone ran her off the road and she hit a power pole. He also told me that the female that was driving was already dead by the time they got to the scene. Darn shame too, they said it looked like she was about eight months pregnant. If you look in the back seat, you can see a bunch of baby stuff like that stuffed bear and that blanket with the pink rosebuds. So, that's how I know it wasn't her driving." The mechanic looked over to where Kalyca had been standing when he said this.

"Huh? Where'd she go? Oh, well. I've got to get back to work. I'm sure she's around here somewhere. Can't get too far on foot."

Jack turned a full circle looking all around for Kalyca. Where did she go? She was just there a minute ago. She wasn't across the street or by his car. He ran around the back to look for the restrooms and knocked on the one marked for ladies. There was no answer. This didn't make sense. Nothing about this day made sense. He walked back to the front and over to his car and got in. She couldn't have gotten far. He turned the key in his ignition and started to pull out onto the road, but in which direction? For some reason, he decided to go back to where he had found her sitting by the road. As he drove out of the city limits, he caught a glimpse of the sign that displayed the town's name from his rearview mirror. The backward writing spelled Mirage. "Okay, this is getting freaky!"

Jack's thoughts spun around in his brain as he drove down the road back to where he found Kalyca. "I must be crazy. If I had any sense I'd just turn back around and continue on my way. Why should I care where this woman went? But Jack knew he did care. For some reason, she appeared out of nowhere in his life today, and then disappeared just as fast. He ran through the conversations they had trying to remember everything she had said to him. There was no way she had driven that vehicle today, because she was very much alive. Her vehicle must still be out there on the highway, just like the mechanic said. But even as he thought this, he knew that in some way she was connected to that vehicle.

He continued to follow along the road that he had been driving when he found Kalyca. Suddenly, the sun disappeared and it started to downpour. The desert faded into the familiar scenery that Jack was used to seeing along the route he traveled. Maybe he just dreamed it all. "Yeah, that's it. I must've gotten a little bit of a sun stroke and imagined everything." Except that when he looked at his gas gauge, it did read full, just like his stomach felt from having lunch, so he couldn't have imagined that.

A sweet aroma filled the air in his car and breathing in deeply, he tried to iden- tify it. As he looked at the mile marker posts along the roadway, he realized that he somehow got turned around and was driving toward Las Vegas once again. He spotted several cars ahead of him through the rainy windshield, and looking in his rearview mirror, behind him also. "Well, I must be on the right track again, with this amount of traffic on the highway. I could swear they weren't there a few minutes ago."

He turned on his CD player and tried to relax as he listened to some tunes. If Kalyca was out here, he certainly couldn't find her and he hoped that someone had given her a ride in this rain. She was definitely different from any other woman he'd met, but now it was time for him to just get home and forget about this day.

The car ahead of him was going too slow for him and he moved up as close as he could to get ready to pass. Just when he was about to pull into the passing lane, he glanced at the plate of the car he was passing. He couldn't believe what he was reading on the license plate; 'Xanadu'. He looked up at the car; it was a blue Ford Taurus. Either this was a coincidence, or this was the same car he left behind at the gas station less than an hour ago. Kalyca's words came back to him, "There are no coincidences, Jack. Just like there are no accidents either."

Jack pulled back into his lane and decided not to pass. The car ahead of him slowed down a little bit more, and signaled as it drove onto the shoulder and parked. Jack followed suit, and parked behind it. He got out of his vehicle and walked over to the driver's side of the car. A woman sat there and rolled down her window as Jack approached her vehicle. She had long auburn hair and when she looked up at him, he could see her turquoise blue eyes. "Kalyca?" Jack smiled as the name left his lips. She looked back at him slightly confused.

"I'm sorry; you must have me mistaken for someone else. Is that why you got so close to my car back there? I'm not used to driving in this kind of weather and it frightened me a little." Jack stood outside the car, looking down at her in the pouring rain, not caring that he was getting soaked. He could see that this woman was not Kalyca, even though she looked very much like her. This woman was very pregnant. He looked into the back seat and saw the teddy bear along with the other baby stuff, including the blanket with the rose bud print.

"I'm sorry about that. I was trying to pass and it's hard to see the oncoming traffic in this rain. I hope you're okay." She smiled at him and nodded her head. "I'm fine now. I was just a little shook up. It looks like the rain is starting to let up, so it should be much better now. What was that name you called me before?" Jack brushed a lock of wet hair out of his eyes as he looked down at this woman who could've been Kalyca's twin. "You look like a woman that I met earlier. Her name was Kalyca...it means..." The woman interrupted him before he could finish. "I know, it means rosebud. By some strange coincidence, when I found out that my baby is going to be a girl, I chose that name for her. I didn't think there were too many women out there that would have that name."

"Lady, if there's one thing I've learned today, it's that there are no coincidences." He nodded to her as he turned to go back to his car. The woman was already driving away as Jack sat down behind the wheel. He recognized the fragrance in his car now, roses. He pushed the button on his navigational screen and instantly it flashed on for him, displaying the route to Las Vegas. As he pulled back onto the road, he hit the speed dial on his cell phone and listened for his secretary's voice.

"Keep the coffee hot, Sheila, I'm coming home. By the way, the next time I have to make this trip, book me a flight."

BELLE'S BAYOU

"I like living on the bayou…'lived here most of my life, nigh on fifteen years now. Ain't no better place in the world in my opinion. People think life is dull out here in alligator swamp land, especially those big city folks up in Baton Rouge or New Orleans. But I disagree…I think there's a lot of life and mystery out here. Why we even had an escaped murderer come through our swamp five years back. He got away from those guards from the prison up North. They were on some kind of clean-up crew when the bayou waters flooded over and we had a whole mess of trees and dead catfish a lyin' around. Well, the convict fellas, they were brought down to help and this guy slipped past the guards during a scare when some alligators crept up looking for food. They were mean—those alligators that year. I guess the floods sort of made them cranky."

Mirabelle Julip was perched upon a tree stump by some willows that she was using for shade from the broiling morning sun. Sprawled on the shaded grass beside her was her younger cousin by one year, Wilhimena, who was called Mena for short. She was visiting Mirabelle, or Belle (we like using the second part of our name in the south) for the summer.

It was just Belle and her mama these days. Her daddy was killed when she was nine years old. He drove a truck to the big cities and delivered catfish, shrimp, and crawfish from the bayou waters to the various businesses. He happened to be in the wrong place at the wrong time one day, when he stopped at a restaurant to drop off a load, unaware that it was being held up at the time. He walked in through the back door of the kitchen just as the gunman was pushing the owner through the doors leading from the dining area. Startled by the unexpected intrusion, the robber, later to be caught and identified as one Jake Reilly, shot his pistol at Belle's daddy, striking him through the heart.

Belle's mama worked at the nursing home in town to support them and Belle would take odd jobs such as cleaning or sewing for extra money for them too. She liked having her cousin visit. It got lonely sometimes when her mama was working.

Mena looked up at Belle as she sat looking upon the water. Her dark curls and facial features were not unlike her own considering their mamas were sisters. The only difference being Belle had her daddy's green eyes while Mena's eyes were brown.

"Did they ever catch him, Belle? The murderer that is…" Mena felt a shudder go through her body and the hairs rise into goose-bumps on her arms. It was as if she thought he'd show himself right then and there, after all these years had gone by since he escaped.

They never did find him Mena but I wouldn't worry too much. Most likely the alligators got him before he got too far. Neither hide nor hair has been seen from him in all this time. They followed his tracks through the mud and they ended at the water's edge about two miles down the river from where he got away. The only way he could've made it across those waters was by swimming and like I said, the alligators were real cranky that year."

Mena looked out at the bayou and decided that she'd had enough of it for one day, and proceeded to get up off the ground. "I think I'll go inside the house and read for awhile, Belle…will you be coming too?"

"Not yet Mena." Belle got up too, but not to go toward the house. "I have some crawfish traps to check in the water first. Mama's gonna make us some Creole crawfish tonight for supper if'n I bring a good catch home. It won't take me long…I'll be along in a little bit."

Mena went back to Belle's house. Belle pulled her canoe out from the shed. She loved that canoe. Her daddy had helped her make it right before he died. He used to take her fishing and hunting on his days off. He taught her how to use a rifle when she was only eight years old.

Belle placed her rifle into the canoe and pushed off into the water as she climbed into the boat. Her thoughts remained on the times she had spent with her daddy on the bayou as she checked each trap and emptied the crawfish into the net she carried in her boat.

Belle looked out upon the murky waters of her beloved bayou. Her daddy had loved it so much and enjoyed sharing his love with Belle. It was moments like this that she missed him the most, but then she would remember that her daddy's soul lived on here in the bayou and as long as the river continued to flow…so would his love. She looked down at the rifle in her boat. She kept it with her for protection against the gators. She had it with her five years ago when she came upon a stranger who needed a ride across the river. She offered to help him and told him to climb into the canoe. The boat moved them along the river as they traveled in silence. The sounds of the bayou were murmuring its song as the river turned into a dark and desolate swamp. Desolate, except for the hungry critters that resided there.

The snapping noises of the gators as they opened and closed their snouts kept the stranger's attention away from Belle. He didn't even hear her pick up the rifle until the sound of the shot going off echoed through the air, and then it was too late.

Belle's thoughts returned to the present as she checked her last trap. The bayou had always been good to her. It gave her food to eat and wonderful memories.

Poor Jake Reilly, the bayou wasn't very good to him. All that blood from the gunshot wound made the gator's fight hard over him. Yep, the alligator's sure were cranky that year…

Dear Abby

With a smudge on his cheek that he was unaware of, he arrived at the door of one Miss Abigail Trueheart, or Abby, as she was known by her friends and family. He was neither, at least not yet anyway. He would like to be a part of her world. One of the many that had the right to call her "Abby".

It was a long journey for him to just get to this moment. The moment when he just had to raise his hand to the door and knock. He never would've believed it possible to even come this far. To be at this door as a visitor and not as the mechanic who dropped her car off after he had done some repair to it.

The first time they met was five years ago. She had just turned sixteen and her daddy bought her a brand new car for her birthday. Her daddy told her to take real good care of it. Being the obedient daughter, she brought it promptly into the service station where Zach worked for the first of many oil changes and check-ups.

He was just out of high school then and had started working full time at the garage. He didn't think there could be any other future for him than the smell of gasoline and oil and scrubbing engine grease from under his finger nails on a daily basis. He resigned himself to this fate until he met Miss Abigail. She was like a breath of fresh air permeating through the car fumes and constant billow of cigarette smoke that hung over the garage from the other chain-smoking mechanics. From the first moment that Zach met her, he knew that he loved her.

Miss Abigail would always smile at Zach and ask him about his day. Even when she went off to college she would still return home on holidays and bring her car in. She would wait there at the garage while he serviced her car and pass the time talking to him about her studies and the people she met. Zach never had much new to say about his life, confined to a dull routine of oil filters and spark plugs. She was the extraordinary in his ordinary life.

After working at the garage for two and a half years, Zach decided to enroll at the local college. He still put in as many hours as he could at the garage to pay for it, fitting in classes and study time. He did it. After four years of long days of working and studying, Zach graduated with a degree in Accounting. He never realized he had it in him. He never thought he'd be anything more than just the mechanic with smudges of grease on his face and hands every time Miss Abigail stopped by with her car.

He interviewed for a job in the accounting department at JB Truehearts, Inc. and got it. Mr. Trueheart was impressed with young Zach. He was efficient and hard working. He invited Zach over for dinner that night with him and his wife and daughter. Along the way, Zach came across old Mrs. Thornhill on the side of the road with a flat tire. He helped her change her tire, unaware that he got some dirt from the tire on his hand, which he got on his face when he brushed back a lock of hair that fell into his eyes while he was leaning down. Mrs. Thornhill was very grateful and Zach assured her he was more than happy to do it for her.

Zach continued on his way to the Truehearts. Here he was now, standing at the door. He raised his hand to knock but the door opened before he got the chance to. Standing before him was Miss Abigail. Her blond hair flowing around her shoulders as she opened the door to Zach. Her blue eyes twinkled as she noted the smudge on Zach's face. "I see that you can take the man out of the garage but…" Zach looked at his face in the mirror by the entry. He was embarrassed by the smudge of dirt on his face. "I helped change Mrs. Thornhill's tire on the way here. I apologize for my appearance, Miss Abigail."

Abby took Zach's arm and led him into the living room. "That's okay, Zach. You look wonderful to me. By the way, you can just call me Abby."

A LITTLE PIECE OF
LEMON CAKE

The rain was falling harder now, forcing Emily to turn on her windshield wipers. She had been driving through a fine mist that day and doing okay, even with the fog that threatened to envelop the highway that she traveled. She hated the squeaking noise the wipers made. She'd have to replace the blades one of these days. Another item to add to her list of things that she'll forget to do.

The fog clouded much of the surrounding scenery, along with the ascending darkness of the approaching nightfall. She imagined that there was a variety of foliage and trees along the mountain road she followed. Isn't that the way it should be in Appalachia country? A far cry from what she left behind in Brooklyn. Contrary to popular belief, more than one tree does grow in Brooklyn, but you wouldn't find too many mountains. The closest thing to a mountain that she'd ever seen there was the large grassy hill in the park across the street from the apartment where she had lived, if living is what you call what she'd been doing for the past six months.

Tears stung her eyes as she thought about that hill in the park, blurring her vision a little more than it was already as she tried to see through the unrelenting downpour. That was Matt's favorite place to play. She could see him now her mind, running down the hill in the summer, tripping and falling in the grass along the way. He'd be laughing all the way down to the bottom where he'd land and jump up and run into her arms. On snowy days in the winter he would trudge to the top with his sled and it would be hours before she could finally bribe him back inside with a large mug of hot chocolate and cookies fresh from the oven…chocolate chip, that was his favorite.

This would be her first summer without him. She had a lot of firsts ahead of her. Mother's Day had been the worst, then there'll be the first Christmas, his birthday, her birthday…all without Matt. It would be almost six months now. She longed to hold him in her arms again. It had been just her and Matt and their cat, Abner, in that small one bedroom apartment that they shared. Now it didn't seem so small anymore. In fact, it seemed to grow bigger and emptier a little more each day.

Emily looked down at the sleeping calico lying on the front seat next to her. "We should be there soon, Abner. If I can just read the signs through this rain." She was looking for the exit that would lead her to Heartville. "What a name for a town, huh Abner? Maybe I can find myself a new heart there, Lord knows I don't seem to have one anymore." Not that she expected any response from the cat, but she would've appreciated it if he would have at least opened an eye to show some interest in the conversation.

The rain was beginning to let up, making it easier to see the road signs. She found the exit she was looking for and followed the directions that she had been given. If they were accurate, it should only be a few more miles. As she was getting closer to what would be her new home, at least for the next twelve months, for that was the amount of time she had agreed upon, she started to question this move. Once again she turned to the cat for consultation. "What are we doing here Abner?" Finally Abner was showing some kind of interest. He actually twitched a whisker. "Yesterday we were in Brooklyn and today we're here in the Appalachian Mountains, somewhere in West Virginia or Georgia for all I know, going to some town called Heartville of all places. Am I nuts?…Of course I'm nuts. I lost my mind when I lost Matt and this is where I wind up. I guess it's better than Belview, or at least I hope it is."

Emily could see the outline of a town ahead of her. She had been driving along a dirt road that seemed to be climbing higher and not going anywhere. There weren't any streetlights that she could see. In fact, the whole town was pitched in darkness, except for one house that had a front porch light on and a light shining in one of its front rooms. It was only ten o'clock in the evening. Didn't anybody stay up to watch the late show anymore? That's if they even have television out here.

She parked her old station wagon in front of the house with the light. She hoped this was the right place. She looked at the mailbox and saw the name "Moore". This must be it. It was an Ida Moore that had written her with directions and who would be renting her a house while she stayed in Heartville. She left Abner sleeping in the car as she got out and stretched her legs. It had been a long drive and she was weary and just wanted a cool bath and a soft bed. She walked around the car to the front of the two-story brick house. She looked down at the sidewalk that she stood on. "Well, at least they don't roll them up at night." She opened the front gate of the white picket fence and approached the front of the house, taking in the flower boxes along the front porch that were filled with flowers that she could only guess the names of. She never had a garden back in Brooklyn. Only the daisies that Matt would pick for her in the park and that she would place in a jelly glass on the dinner table. She climbed the two steps that went up to the porch and stood in front of the screen door as she rang the bell.

She didn't have to wait long for a response. The door opened and she found herself face to face with the woman whom she assumed to be Ida Moore. She looked to be in her early sixties, with hair that seemed as if it had once been a honey blond, taken over by silvery strands, which seemed to be the predominant color now. She wore silver glasses over what looked like eyes the color of a blue summer sky. She had on a summer dress made of a flower print which reminded Emily of the flower boxes on the front porch. Emily shook her head as if it were filled with cobwebs that needed clearing out. Why were these thoughts going through her head? Comparing someone's eyes to a summer sky? It had to be this place. Ever since she started driving into the Appalachians her mind would wander off on these offbeat tangents. She even pulled the car over that morning to admire the view of the mountains from a look out point along the highway.

Ida was the first to speak. "Hello dear, you must be Emily Phillips. We were starting to get a little worried when it got so late and you hadn't arrived yet. The fog rolls in pretty fast at night here in the mountains. I'm glad that you finally made it." Emily was entranced by Ida's southern accent. It was soft and melodic. She wondered what the people of Heartville would think of her accent. Not that anyone from Brooklyn really had an accent of course. "The fog and rain slowed me down a bit, but it let up enough for me to find my way here. Your directions were right on the mark. It will be nice to get settled in for the night, so if you'll just tell me where I'm to live…" Ida looked at her as if she were studying her. Emily didn't have to imagine what she saw when she looked at her. She had been on the road for two days. Her jeans were tattered and her white tee shirt had a coffee stain on it from when she spilled it that afternoon. Drinking and driving really isn't safe, especially with a hot cup of coffee in one hand and the steering wheel in the other. Her feet were dusty under the sandals that she wore and her short auburn hair was damp with sweat. Her gray eyes were red from the strain of driving and the tears that stung them earlier.

Ida reached out and touched Emily on the shoulder. Emily flinched, not used to any human contact in the past six months. This did not dissuade Ida, though, as she kept her hand on Emily's shoulder and guided her into the house, closing the screen door behind them. "There's plenty of time for that. You need to sit down and rest a bit first. I have some nice cold iced tea and some lemon cake in the kitchen. You look like you need to put a little more meat on your bones, dear. You're as thin as a toothpick! Come on in and meet my husband Boyd and have some refreshments, and then Boyd will show you where you'll be staying. It's just down the street. It was my mama's house until last spring when she passed away. I had been thinking about selling it until I heard that they were hiring a new schoolteacher to come out and replace Mr. Gillespie, after he had to retire after his heart attack. The minister asked the congregation if anyone had a place available for the new teacher and Boyd and I were the first to raise our hand and offer Mama's house. Of course, later on if you decide you like the house, we'd be happy to still sell it to ya."

Emily followed Ida through the living room toward the kitchen. The living room was large, with a fireplace and what looked like a hundred pictures of people, young and old, all across the mantle. There was a large quilt hanging over the back of the sofa and a wooden rocker by the large bay window, positioned in the right place to look out at the street. As they approached the kitchen, Emily heard a man's voice calling to Ida. "Is that our new tenant you got there Ida?" Ida nudged Emily ahead of her into the kitchen.

Emily had never seen a kitchen like this before in her life. It was larger than her whole apartment had been. There were large oak cabinets at one end, with huge counter space she would've killed for in her small kitchen in Brooklyn. At the other end was a long wooden table with eight chairs surrounding it. The table was in front of a wall made up entirely of windows that looked out into the back yard and surrounding mountains. A man got up from the table as she came into the room and reached out his hand to her. "You must be Emily. I'm Boyd. I bet you're hot and thirsty. Why don't you sit right down. Ida has some iced tea and some fine lemon cake for you."

Emily shook Boyd's hand. She had to stretch her neck to look up at his face. He was a great deal taller than her, she being only 5'4" and he seemed at least 6'3". His hair was all gray and he had brown eyes that seemed to hold some happy secret as he led her to the table. She would never know that secret that would make her eyes shine like that. "This really isn't necessary. I don't want to keep you from going to bed. Just show me where I'll be staying and I'll be on my way." As if they couldn't hear a word she said, Boyd sat down across from her at the table and Ida proceeded to pour her a glass of iced tea. She placed it in front of Emily along with a plate that contained two pieces of what must be lemon cake. "Nonsense, dear. We'll get to bed soon enough…you just eat and don't you worry none." Knowing she was fighting a losing battle, Emily picked up the glass of tea and started to sip, but eventually gulped down half the glass of what was probably the best iced tea she had ever tasted.

She really didn't think she could eat any cake. She didn't eat much these days. She would have to remind herself some days to perform what used to be routine for her and Matt. Getting up, brushing your teeth, eating…some days she would just forget. Especially the days she forgot to get up; when she pulled the covers back over her head and stayed in bed. She picked up the fork and took a bite of the cake. It melted in her mouth. Before she knew it, she had finished the first piece and was already halfway through the second. She looked up in time to catch a glimpse of Boyd and Ida smiling at each other across the table.

"Thank you, that was really good. Now I'd really like to get settled for the night, and I left Abner sleeping in the car." Ida gasped as she put her hand up to her chest. "Oh, my dear, I didn't realize you had your son with you in the car. We must bring him right in and give him something, too." Ida started to get up but Emily put her hand on her arm to stop her. "Abner is not my son; he's my cat. I left him curled up in the front seat of the car." Ida sat back in her chair and looked at Emily. "Well, that's a relief. Then where is your son? Is he staying with someone until you get settled in? I remember the minister mentioning that you had written on your application that you had a five year old boy."

Emily could feel that familiar knot forming in her stomach. That familiar coldness sinking in. Her eyes once again stung with tears as she looked away from Ida and Boyd and pretended to admire a clay pot that was on top of a shelf along the wall. She knew the words were there, but to say them made real what she didn't want to be real. Finally she took a deep breath and turned to Ida. "Last year when I applied for the teaching job, I did have a son. He died about six months ago. Now I'm really tired and would really like to get to bed." Boyd and Ida looked at each other. They both had seen the pain in Emily's eyes. Ida got up and cleared off the dishes. "Of course, dear, it is getting late. Come on Boyd, let's show her the house, and then you can help her carry her belongings in."

* * * * * *

The sun was stretching its rays across the mountains as Emily sat on a wooden swing on the front porch of her house. Wrapped in her terry bathrobe, for the mornings could be quite cool even in summer here, she sipped a mug of hot coffee as she gazed upon the scene before her. This would be number six. She woke up early on her first morning in her new home, and, not being able to fall back to sleep, arose and came out on the porch to witness probably her first sunrise ever, or at least the first one like this. Now six days later, it still seemed new and different each time. Everything seemed to replenish itself daily and each new dawn brought new life to the mountains. How could life continue to go on without Matt?…

It didn't take too long to unpack what little belongings she had brought with her. The house came with furniture, and a kitchen that was not quite as large as Ida's but still bigger than she'd ever had before. Abner had already found his perfect sleeping spot on a cushioned window seat in the living room. The Moores' had been very helpful in getting her settled in. They showed her where the general store was in town, for groceries or whatever other items she may need. Definitely not anything like her supermarket where she shopped back in Brooklyn. It was more personal. You didn't need an express line because there was only one register and the people would just chat with each other while they waited for their turn. She went to the school to meet the principal and was given her lessons that she would be teaching when school commenced again in three weeks.

Today was Sunday and considered a big social day from what Ida told her. Everyone went to the same Presbyterian church that stood in the middle of town. After their noon meals the men would go off, and either fish or just sit around and tell stories, while their wives got together and canned or sewed quilts, keeping one eye on the children as they ran about playing. It sounded pretty boring to Emily and she decided to just stay around the house by herself. She didn't feel like socializing and answering a lot of questions that the other women would be sure to ask. She knew that Ida and Boyd would be disappointed but she didn't really care about that. She didn't owe them anything but their monthly rent for the house.

*   *   *   *

The sun was high in the sky as Emily worked on her front porch, struggling to place flowers in some window boxes she had found in the garage. She hadn't planned on planting any, thinking it useless to try and turn this house into a home. She came upon some daisies while walking through the woods the other day and she felt the need to bring some home with her and put them in a jelly glass and place them on the kitchen table. That led her to the general store in search of some more daisies that she could replant and place around the front porch.

Lost in her own thoughts while patting down the soil around the flowers, she didn't hear Ida approach until she was walking up the porch steps. "Good afternoon Emily, we missed you at church today." Emily turned her back to Ida after greeting her and continued working with the flowers. "You can't miss what you never had and you'll never have my butt in that church, lady!" Emily expected to see shock in Ida's eyes when she turned to face her and was surprised to see her smiling instead. For a second she glimpsed a sadness in her eyes behind the silver glasses but then it was gone again. Ida moved over to the wooden swing to sit down and looked up at Emily. "How did it happen, dear?"

Emily knew what Ida was asking. She opened her mouth to tell her to mind her own business but the words wouldn't come. Instead she sat down cross-legged across from Ida, on the porch floor, leaning against the railing. "I taught first grade at the elementary school in our neighborhood in Brooklyn. I was so excited when Matt was finally old enough to attend and we could walk to school together each day. It was just the two of us you know. My boyfriend took off when he found out I was pregnant with Matt." Emily paused to look over at Ida expecting to see some kind of disapproval in her eyes, but there was none. Her thoughts returned to those walks with Matt and her eyes began to glisten as she remembered how much she enjoyed them. "One day, in the middle of a spelling lesson, I heard a gun shot. The kids were all excited but I calmed them down, convincing them it was probably just a film someone was showing in one of the other class rooms. A few minutes later the principal came into the room with a teacher's aide to take over my class. I knew then something was terribly wrong."

Emily began to shake as she continued talking, turning away from Ida to stare out at the mountains. "I couldn't hear a word he was saying as we walked down the hall to Matt's kindergarten room. When we came to the door, I saw that the classroom was empty except for the school nurse kneeling next to Matt, who was lying on the floor. I ran over to him and saw that he was bleeding from his chest. I could hear the ambulance siren blaring outside as I picked up his hand and held it up to my face." Ida reached out and put her hand on Emily's shoulder. She didn't flinch this time, either unaware of it or needing the comfort of human touch at that moment. "He opened his eyes and looked up at me and said 'Mommy'. I felt the life go out of him as his eyes closed for the last time." Emily stopped talking. They both sat there in silence for what seemed like hours but were only minutes, watching a flock of birds dancing in the sky above them.

Emily stood up and wrapped her arms around one of the porch columns, needing something for them to hold. "What kind of God allows one little boy to shoot another little boy?....allows one child to kill another child?" Tears flowed freely from Emily's eyes; she could not keep them in check anymore. She didn't want to. She turned to see the questioning look in Ida's eyes. She swiped the tears from her cheek with her hand before she spoke again. "One of Matt's class mates thought it would be cool to bring in his father's gun for show and tell. The teacher was shocked by what the child was holding and reached out for him to give it to her. The boy didn't want to give up his toy and pulled away causing the gun to go off in his hand. The bullet struck Matt in the chest."

Ida nodded, understanding what happened now. She patted the seat next to her on the swing, motioning for Emily to sit next to her. Emily hesitated for a second and then sat down next to Ida, carefully moving to one side so as to not have any physical contact with her.

Ida understood and a sad smile reached her eyes as she looked out at the mountains that surrounded her and Emily. "We didn't always live in town here, Boyd and I, that is. We used to live up farther in the mountains a ways where we had a farm. Our first two children were girls and we loved them dearly but Boyd was overjoyed when our third child came along and was a boy. We named him Jamie. He was the liveliest thing you'd ever seen. Boyd would work the fields and the girls were off at school and it would be just Jamie and me. He was four by then and followed me everywhere on the farm.

"I remember that year we were having trouble with wild dogs getting into our chickens. One afternoon while Jamie was napping, I heard noise coming from the chicken coop and I was worried that some of those wild dogs had come into our yard. I grabbed the rifle off the wall and loaded it and walked out to the back yard. Sure enough, there were dogs there. They caught wind of me and started growling. I didn't see Jamie wake up from his nap and come looking for me. He saw the dogs in the yard and, wanting to play with them, started running toward them just as I had taken my first shot…" Emily stopped Ida from saying anything more by placing a hand on her shoulder. She knew what the rest would be.

The two women sat there like that for a long time staring out at the mountains. No words were necessary. At that moment their hearts and thoughts were one. They both knew God didn't cause a little boy to kill another little boy or a mother to accidentally shoot her child. It was a cruel twist of fate that sometimes happens in life. Looking out at the mountains, they saw what God gave back to those who lose so much. Life did start anew each day here and their children would always be alive in their hearts. Maybe this was the right name for the town.

Emily looked over at Ida and smiled for the first time in six months. " I baked yesterday, following that recipe you wrote out for me. How would you like to come inside and have a glass of iced tea and a little piece of lemon cake?" Ida looked back toward the mountains one more time before nodding. The two women got up from the swing and went inside.

THE INNER CIRCLE

It was the eve of the "Vernal Equinox". That moment in time when everything seems magically balanced in the Universe…when everything seems to be in perfect alignment, day and night being of equal length. Sam's old physics professor at Yale used to say that he believed it was an exceptionally prolific moment in nature. "Science influenced by the spiritual essences of nature marking the onset of a new season, bringing about a new feeling of hope." Sam smiled at the memory of his old professor's words. He had learned a lot from his mentor, hoping to help save the world someday with this knowledge.

That was a long time ago for Sam Tarmon, and the hope was still there, however, he hoped to save himself first, before he could start on the world. The past ten years weighed heavily upon his soul. Too many battles were fought by him. Too many friends lost forever to the cause, whatever the cause may have been at the time.

It was a quiet night. The influence of spring evident among the flowers and leaves, erupting through the forest where Sam walked. A rustling could be heard now and then, making him aware but not too concerned. Sam gazed up at the heavens as he walked. He did not need his flashlight this evening, though he did carry it. There was an abundance of stars and the moon was almost full. The combination provided enough light for Sam to find his way.

Though the moonlight cast eerie shadows where Sam walked, he wasn't frightened. An ex Navy Seal, he was well skilled in the art of self-defense. He was tall, about 6'2" and weighed a little over 200 lbs…enough to pull his own weight in any fight, especially with a stiletto in his boot and a 9mm automatic under his right arm.

The denim jacket he wore over his T-shirt and jeans was no match for the brisk breeze, but it didn't bother him. The cool air was invigorating out here on this Cornish moor. He continued along the path, relishing the serenity of the moment. He cherished these peaceful interludes as treasures whenever he was gifted with them.

He flew to Cornwall from Belfast, and arrived just a few hours ago. He couldn't wait to explore the Cornish countryside. He was told of its mystical Celtic background by an old buddy from his military past. His friend Danny was originally from here, before his family migrated to the states when he was a child. He had wonderful memories and stories of Cornwall that he shared with Sam. He'd always say that he and Sam would have to come here one day together when they were on leave. Danny was gone now and Sam didn't think he'd ever want to go without him.

He changed his mind when his recent mercenary duties brought him to Ireland. A wealthy Irish businessman hired him to intercede when shipments of cargo for his factory were constantly being intercepted and stolen before arriving at his warehouse outside of Belfast. Sam succeeded in tracking down the culprit behind the thefts and received a nice bonus from the very grateful Irishman. Sam traced the looting operation to a manager at the factory. Sympathetic to a group of Irish terrorists, he used the money from the stolen shipments to further their cause.

Since Sam was so close to England, he relented and decided to come to Cornwall. He thought about Danny, walking this same path that he tread upon, and could almost feel his buddy walking along with him.

His thoughts constantly returned to the years he spent with his close buddies. There were six of them. They had all gone through basic together and were the best in their unit. Together they made one hell of a special task force for the Seals...so why was he the only one left now?...

The missions they had been sent on were always dangerous, but they got the job done and came back alive. All six of them, never leaving anyone behind. For five years they were the conquering heroes. When a situation seemed hopeless, the military sent their team in.

The last mission Sam and his men were sent on was five years ago in North Africa. A US military camp, set up as an intermediary in an arms exchange, was raided by Iranian militants. The transactions were usually illegal trade-offs between third world nations. The United States set up camp to keep an eye on the situation and make sure these weapons didn't get into the wrong hands. Once they determined who was behind the procurement and selling of these weapons, they would be eliminated in the most discreet way possible.

When the Iranians took over, it was during a negotiation scam that the US set up with some buyers. The camp had contraband arms in their possession at the time. Out of the fifty soldiers stationed there, twenty had been killed and the other thirty held hostage. It was one of those hopeless situations that called for their special team. The odds were stacked against the six of them, but they were good at what they did and they were, as always, ready for the challenge. Something went wrong though, a leak somewhere along the line. The Iranians knew they were coming and an ambush had been set. The memories of his buddies covered in blood, body parts strewn about, still invaded his dreams at night.

He woke up on a hospital ship in the Mediterranean after being in a coma for three days. It was then that he was told he had been the only survivor of his unit. He was the sniper for the team, which placed him far enough away from the explosions. The doctor aboard the ship assured him of a full recovery. All limbs and fingers were accounted for, the only evidence of the encounter being a large slash under his left eye caused by flying shrapnel from a claymore mine. He would carry a scar because of it to remind him of all he lost that day. He would carry many more unseen scars that would live with him for many years to come.

Sam brought his hand up to his face to brush aside some stray brown strands of hair blowing in his eyes. He wore his hair longer now that he was no longer in the military. It was almost to his shoulders and strands of gray started appearing here and there, making him look a little older, if not wiser, for his 32 years.

His fingers touched the deep scar under his left eye. He had gray eyes that could turn the color of steel when he was angry or become the blue of a crystal lake at moments like this, when he felt calm and as near to content that was possible for him, especially when his mind was invaded by unwanted memories.

Sam found an old tree stump along the path he followed, and decided to sit down for a short rest. His thoughts continued their journey back to the past as he looked down at the tattoo on his left bicep. He had removed his jacket so as to get the full effect of the Cornish breezes. It was a tattoo that he and his teammates all had worn on their arms as a symbol of their comradeship. It was the standard Navy Seal insignia, with an anchor placed in front of a seal, but they had also added each other's initials for good luck.

The military leak leading to the fatal ambush was traced to a CIA agent named Randall Douglas. He remembered Randall well from back in basic. He didn't quite have the "stuff" to be a Navy Seal, so he was transferred to a different branch of the military, which eventually led to his position with the C I A.

Randall held a deep hatred for the Seals because of his failure to become one, and especially resented Sam's elite team. He was paid very handsomely from third world governments for his assistance on their illegal arms dealings. He was instrumental in the take over of the military camp in North Africa. He knew they would send in the special Seal task force and passed the word on what route Sam's team would be taking into the camp.

Sam left the military after that. Even knowing that Randall's duplicity was discovered, leading to his subsequent court martial and death sentence, did not bring him the peace he sought. Too many wounds still needed to heal.

Sam decided to become a mercenary. A man for hire to anyone willing to pay the right price for the right cause. He would put his fate in his own hands and choose his own battles.

Sam decided that it was time to move on; not only physically as he got up from the stump, but spiritually as well. "The past is gone," he thought, " and can't be changed. What good does it do to dwell on it?"

He put his jacket back on and took a path that led to one of the many Cornish dolmens that inhabited the moors. The innkeeper from where he was staying had given him directions on how to find it. Danny had played there many times as a child, and Sam was curious to explore this place. Danny had explained to him that Cornwall carried many ancient monuments, such as dolmens, which consisted of a circle of upright stones supporting a horizontal slab. He claimed that they held sacred powers that lent mystery to the Cornish moors. Sam always laughed at him. "I'll show you someday, Sammy, and then we'll see who laughs!" Danny would get a certain look in his eyes when he'd say this to Sam as, if they held some secret. Then he'd smile and pat Sam on the back and say "Someday, Sammy, someday..."

According to the innkeeper, the dolmen, which he called "Boscawen-un", was hidden in a field somewhere along this road. Sam moved onward, unable to see anything yet. An eerie mist was starting to form. If Sam didn't know better, he'd almost believe that Danny was creating these special effects for him from the grave. It was getting harder to see now, so he turned on his flashlight. After walking further into the mist, he finally found what he had been searching for, and was mesmerized by what he saw.

Sam was surrounded by a circle of stones. They just appeared out of the mist, as if he had summoned them. He used his flashlight to study them more closely. There was one stone that was made out of quartz, a stone considered highly sacred by the Celts. Sam touched the stone and felt an electrical surge shoot up his arm. He pulled his hand away quickly, but not before a numbness had set in. Suddenly, there was a buzzing sound, as if the stones were vibrating. It continued to get louder. Sam covered his ears with his hands trying, to block out the piercing noise. Memories of his buddies dying invaded his mind. He could hear the sound of the explosions echoing in his head. A bright light flashed in his eyes, and then there was darkness.

✻   ✻   ✻   ✻

Shades of lilac and orange painted the sky as the sun awakened to another dawn, leaving behind the last dregs of darkness. Birds fluttered across treetops as they espied someone sleeping in the forest, hidden among the leaves from other earth bound travelers. The early morning light enveloped her as she started to stir from her slumber. It caressed her fiery hair like a halo, giving her an ethereal appearance, as if she were a wood nymph or sprite.

The cold morning air chilled her, attesting to the fact that she was indeed of human flesh and blood. Her name was Brigit, given to her by her mother in reverence to the Goddess of fire. "The name does suit you, my sweet darling, considering that mane of flames you carry upon your head, and the temper to go with it." Her mother would say this as she lovingly combed Brigit's hair each night as they sat by the hearth in their hut. Brigit could feel the love from her mother's fingers flow through the brush as she stroked her hair.

Tears formed in Brigit's eyes at the memory. Her mother, along with her father, were both gone now. Her village had been destroyed by Warriors who stole and murdered in the name of their king. King Arawn claimed all the land that his warriors could steal for him as part of his kingdom. He appointed himself as ruler and created his own laws. Laws that were to be obeyed by all but his men, and of course, himself.

Many of the surrounding clans tried to fight these evil demons, but they did not succeed. They were no match for the cunning and heartless soldiers.

When the Warriors came to her village, Brigit had been in the forest gathering herbs for her mother. Her mother was a healer and had taught Brigit in the ways of healing. When she returned to her home late in the afternoon, it was to find nothing but empty, burned out shells where there once had been thatched huts. Smoke and cinders, where children once played.

She found the bodies of her parents near the road that led to the forest. Many of the people from her village were able to escape to the forest…many were not, her family among them. The blacksmith, who had returned to the village to gather what remained of his belongings, helped her bury them. He invited her to join him and his family on their journey to find another home, but she declined. She had a long journey of her own. A quest to find the man responsible for such devastation, and destroy him. It seemed a mighty task for a maiden of eighteen to embrace on her own, but she wasn't afraid. She had nothing more to lose, and she needed a reason to continue to live.

Brigit prayed every night to "Aerone", the Goddess of war. "Please give me the courage and strength to guide me on this journey that I have charted for myself. Send me someone to lead me and help me in my effort to see my parents' death avenged and to stop this evil once and for all!" Brigit repeated this plea each night before she went to sleep in the forest, hidden among the brush.

This morning, Brigit felt her spirits lifted for the first time since her parents' death two months ago. She awoke with a feeling of hope. Her dreams had been filled with the image of a dark haired warrior. She remembered hearing stories as a child of a legendary hero called "Cu Chulainn". He would appear from the mists when all seemed hopeless. He fought giants and dragons and rid the land of evil.

Brigit felt new hope arising from her dreams. She was sure that Aerona was answering her prayers. She would send a warrior to aid Brigit in her quest.

Brigit unwrapped her cloak that she used as a bed at night, where she slept hidden among the leaves. She had removed her woolen tunic before going to sleep and folded it carefully to use as a pillow, and slept only in her linen under tunic. She picked up a small bundle containing the meager belongings she was able to salvage from the ruins of her home. Her mother's brush, a pouch of salves and dried herbs, some small slivers of soap left over from a supply her mother had last made from the flowers of juniper berries and comfrey, and a spare under tunic had been left untouched by the scorching flames. They had been left outside the hut wrapped in an embroidered linen cloth, in anticipation of Brigit's return from her day of herb gathering in the forest. Her mother knew she liked to bathe after a day of foraging among the plants, and had left everything gathered together in the cloth, which would be used to dry herself, by the stream near the edge of the woods.

Brigit walked to a nearby pond for her daily bath. The early morning mists concealed her from prying eyes, should anyone happen upon her. She removed her under tunic and shift, leaving only her knife that she carried strapped to her leg with a leather thong. This she left on for protection against any wild animal that roamed the forest, be it two-legged or four-legged. The water was cold but

Brigit adapted to it quickly enough to enjoy the invigorating cleansing, not only of her body but of her soul as well. She felt something new in the world today, a new beginning. It was the first day of spring and the flowers were in bloom throughout the land. She lathered up her body from one of her bars of soap and then dived completely under the water to rinse herself. She emerged feeling refreshed, brushing her wet hair away from her eyes. She had inherited her mother's beauty and her father's stature, towering over many of the men of her village. She had a narrow waist and an ample bosom, which caught many an eye, as she walked through the town. Her face consisted of a small nose that turned upward at the tip and a full sensuous mouth. The streaks of sunlight that danced upon the water reflected the turquoise of Brigit's eyes. Her eyes sparkled; especially when she was full of mischief, as her mother was want to say many times over again. "What cunning are ye up to this time, wee darling, with your eyes all aglow?" "Don't be thinking ye can fool your mother like ye do your father with that angelic smile of yours." It was at this moment that her mother would hold her hand out waiting for Brigit to give her whatever she was hiding behind her back or in her pocket. Once it was a mouse she had planned to use to scare the blacksmith's wife, who had scolded her for knocking over the milk pail while playing with the other children. Another time it was some prickly woundwort leaves that she planned to hide in her brother's cot.

Brigit's eyes misted over as her thoughts turned to her brother. They had lost him several years past, when he was in his fourteenth year. King Arawn had just begun his reign of terror, and her brother Dunae joined a band of soldiers, against her parents' wishes, who thought him too young, to try and stop the king and his army.

The men were never heard from again, including her brother. Word had eventually found its way to their village of their valiant efforts to fight the king's men, but they were too greatly outnumbered. There had been one or two survivors from other clans that had somehow escaped, missing a limb or two, who had carried tales of the battles they had fought.

Dunae was two years her senior, and would have been a full-grown man today if he had lived. She wished he was there to help her in her cause, for now he would have been better prepared as a warrior than a mere boy of fourteen would've been.

Brigit looked about the grove as she prepared to leave the water. Seeing no one about, she climbed onto the sandy shore and patted herself dry with the linen cloth. She quickly put on her shift and under tunic. She pulled on her woolen tunic of a sapphire blue that contrasted well with her black under tunic. The blue of her gown intensified the color of her eyes and the copper highlights of her hair that she plaited, hanging down the length of her back to her waist. She wore a strand of amber beads around her neck that Dunae had made for her when she was a child. She kept them close to her heart as a remembrance, along with her mother's brush, and the knife that she wore on her thigh that was given to her by her father. These were tokens of the family that she once had, but they could not compare to the memories she held dear in her heart.

She ate a small breakfast of a crust of bread left over from a loaf given to her two days ago by an old woman who lived alone in a thatched hut hidden along the hillside. So hidden in fact, she practically walked into a wall before realizing what it was. The woman invited her to stay for the night and provided her with a loaf of bread and a small slab of goat cheese before she left. She returned the favor by supplying the woman with some medicinal herbs for brewing into tea and a salve to comfort her ailing bones.

Brigit was out of food now, and would have to hunt for a rabbit sometime today, for she desperately longed for a piece of meat to chew on. She was tired of eating plants and wanted something more substantial to ease the hunger pains in her stomach.

Gathering her cloak about her and putting on her leather slippers, she tied her belongings back into the cloth and continued on her way. The sun was beginning to streak through the mists with a promise of a glorious day. She was told of the existence of a place north of here from a passing traveler that visited her village a few years back. He described it as a mystical place where dragons and unicorns once roamed. It was built thousands of years ago by a tribe of people who were fascinated with the earth mother, which was most sacred to them, and her relationship with the sun and the moon. Her parents had laughed at the tales, but Brigit was most curious about this place that the traveler described as a field of flowers surrounded by a circular gate of enormous stones that looked as if they grew out of the ground.

Brigit decided that this would be the place where she would stop for the night since, it would be early evening before she arrived there, if she did not dally too much along the way. Who knows what wonders awaited her there?

A light drizzle began to fall as Brigit approached the stone monument. Luck had been with her today, as she was able to trap a rabbit for her supper this evening. She had gone with her brother many times when they were children to hunt for rabbits in the woods and fish for their supper in the stream near their home. She was grateful for the lessons he had taught her in setting a trap and then using her sling that she carried in her pocket to slay the animal. Her thoughts, as well as her stomach, were eagerly anticipating a warm fire in the shelter of the stones, with the smoky aroma of roasting meat permeating the air. She had walked far today and she was weary from her lonely trek.

The sun dipped low as twilight engulfed the horizon, presenting an eerie mist that surrounded Brigit as she slowly moved into the inner circle of stones. She was entranced by what her eyes beheld. She had never seen anything like it before. She wouldn't have been surprised if a Unicorn appeared from behind one of the columns, so magical did it all seem to her. As she walked around the inner circle, she was startled by a soft sound that she could not name. It was harder to see now since the sun had completely disappeared and the mist grew thicker. She stood still and listened very carefully until she thought she knew from whence the sound had come, and walked toward it. She had only walked a short distance before she tripped over something on the ground and landed on her hands and knees. She was just trying to stand back up when her eyes caught sight of what looked like a man's foot, covered in some kind of strange footwear she did not recognize. Her eyes followed the foot to a leg and then another leg and continued to take in the entire person of a man lying on the ground, sleeping. Her breath caught as she beheld his face. He was the man from her dreams of the past night. She could tell he was a tall man, even lying down as he was. He appeared very muscular, even though his limbs were covered by some odd looking light blue cloth, in such a fashion she could not identify. She did not know how long she sat there next to him on the ground studying his wardrobe before she looked up at his face once again. She was surprised to see gray eyes staring back at her.

✳   ✳   ✳   ✳

Sam's head ached as he opened his eyes. He did not know where he was at the moment, or how he even got here. All he knew was that someone who looked very much like an angel was leaning over him and examining him very closely. Was he dead? Could this be heaven? No, it was too dark to be heaven, and too cold to be hell.

"Where am I?" Sam's voice sounded hoarse. He could barely get the words out. Brigit removed a wooden cup from her herb pouch.

"I will be right back with water for you. There is a brook just across the field." Brigit had run off before Sam could get the words out to stop her. A few minutes passed when he saw her returning from the other side of the clearing. Brigit knelt down next to Sam on the ground. He was sitting up now, trying to shake the cobwebs from his head. At least that's what it felt like to him.

"Here, drink this." She handed Sam the cup and watched him as he drained it of its contents.

Sam cleared his throat and made another attempt at talking, with much better results this time. "Thank you." Sam looked around and realized that he was still at the dolmen in Cornwall. That eased his mind a bit, but why did everything still seem so different? Why was this woman wearing such strange clothing? "Who are you?…What's happened to me?"

Brigit listened carefully to the man's words. He was not of this land, she was sure of that. The strange clothes he wore, and his accent were not known to her. "I am Brigit. You were lying here on the ground sleeping when I came upon you. Did Aerone send you to me? Are you the great warrior Cu-Chulainn?"

"I don't know any Aerone, and my name is definitely not Cu-Choo-choo, or whatever it was you called me. My name is Sam." Sam got up slowly from the ground. He still felt a little shaky, but his head was clear now, and he stood up and looked around the monument and then once again turned to Brigit. "What are you doing here and why are you wearing that weird get-up?"

Brigit was confused by his words. "Get up? I don't understand. What is—how did you say it…weird get-up?"

Sam touched the front of her cloak and folded it back to display the tunics that she wore. "I'm talking about the clothes you 're wearing. Why are you wearing those clothes?"

Brigit brushed his hand away. "I am wearing clothes, sir, so that I don't freeze to death. If you think that odd, then I suggest you look upon your own person. The clothing that you inhabit does not seem fit enough to keep out the merest drafts, and I can honestly say that no one else in this kingdom has ever seen or worn such a costume. I can't even recognize what cloth was used to make this odd apparel."

It was hard for Sam to concentrate on what Brigit was saying to him. The combination of her sultry voice and lilting brogue drove him to distraction. Either he was still suffering some ill effects from the dizziness that came upon him, or this woman, or should he say girl, because she looked like a teenager, was daft. "It's called denim…look, I don't know what's going on here, but I just want to go back to the inn where I was staying and take a hot bath and eat something before I collapse again, from hunger this time."

Brigit looked at Sam and started to have doubts that he was the warrior she had prayed for. "Sir, you are quite mistaken. There is no inn near here, and the only bath you'll be getting is a cold one in the brook across the field. I happen to have a rabbit that I caught for my supper that I would be happy to share with you. That should ease your hunger.

An hour had passed and Sam sat quietly across the fire that Brigit had started. He couldn't believe that she didn't just use matches. She actually used some rocks for making sparks and then added sticks to catch the sparks and stirred it into a roaring flame, adding more wood to keep it going through the night. He then watched her pull a knife from under her dress, and skin the rabbit that she had caught and prepare it for the meal. She added herbs from some kind of pouch that she carried, and placed the rabbit over the fire with some branches to let it cook. He had to admit it smelled delicious, and his stomach growled in response to the aroma. Brigit looked up at him and smiled. She was a beauty. Sam never found a woman that he really felt close to. His relationships usually never lasted longer than a few months, and he liked it that way. He didn't want any long-term commitments, especially in his line of work. It was better to have no attachments and be free to do the job, without worrying about a wife at home. Sam studied Brigit as she tended the meat by the fire. The glowing flames highlighted her features, especially her hair. It looked so silky and shiny that Sam almost reached out his hand to touch it, but thought better of it. She looked young, too young for him.

"The meat is just about done."

Brigit's words brought Sam out of his reverie. "It smells delicious. I could eat a horse right now, but I'll settle for the rabbit."

The last traces of darkness hovered as the sun struggled to break through the early morning mist. Sam awakened from a restless night to find Brigit snuggled against him, still asleep. She had made a bed for them out of leaves and used her cloak as a blanket. Sam had slept in worse places during his tour as a seal, and this was luxury compared to those. He never had a warm, soft body lying next to him in any of the other primitive sleeping accommodations that he had to make do with.

Sam fought the urge to stretch. He didn't want to make a move in fear of awakening Brigit. He looked down at her face as he watched her as she slept. He could feel her warm breath tickle his neck like a soft caress.

As he lay there, his thoughts turned to the events of the previous day. He still found it too incredible to believe. After they had finished eating, Sam decided that he'd had enough of the mystical Cornish moors for one day, and decided to return to the inn. "That was delicious, thank you." Brigit looked up from tending the fire and nodded at Sam. "I was honored to share, I hope your hunger has been appeased." Sam smiled at her as he helped her add more wood to the fire.

"Yes, it has been, but now the only demand my body makes of me now is a soft bed, which is waiting for me back at the inn where I'm staying."

Brigit packed away her leather pouch and stood up as she looked at Sam. "…and where is this inn that you say you have a soft bed awaiting you?" Sam also stood up and pointed to the path that he had taken that day to the dolmen. "Just down that road a little ways, on the other side of the forest." Brigit looked at where Sam was pointing and shook her head. "Nay, I have passed through that way today, and I assure you that I did not come across an inn."

Sam was getting angry now. "Okay lady, I've had enough of this game that you seem to enjoy playing with me. If you'll follow me right now, I will show you where this invisible inn is located."

Brigit was becoming anxious. Though the moon was almost full, the darkness still permeated the night, and she did not relish leaving the warmth of the fire just yet. "Sir…"

Sam interrupted her. "My name is Sam, not sir!"

Brigit hesitated for a moment then continued. "Sir…I mean Sam, it would not be wise to journey through the forest at this time of night. It may not be safe, and it is easy to lose one's direction in the darkness."

"Never fear, my lady." Sam performed an exaggerated bow before Brigit. "I will protect you with my life. Shall we go?" Brigit looked doubtful but decided it would not be wise to defy this man. She gathered her things together while Sam threw dirt on the fire until it was completely extinguished.

They walked together in silence as they made their way through the forest, until they arrived at the clearing where the inn should have been. Sam stopped short, causing Brigit to collide into him. "I must've been mistaken, it must be farther than I thought…", but even as he said this, instinct told him otherwise. For the first time since he had awakened among the stones of the dolmen, Sam studied his surroundings. Everything seemed different to him. The landscape was more ragged and primitive. The trees and plants seemed different from what they had been earlier. Something Danny had once said to him came forward in his mind. "The dolmens of Cornwall are magical, Sammy. Many claim to have had strange experiences when standing among them, including electric shocks or visions. Some even believed that they had actually traveled to another dimension in time. Imagine that Sammy, being able to travel through time!"

Sam had scoffed at Danny's words. It was ludicrous to even consider the concept of time travel. Sam's thoughts returned to the present…or was it? He looked at Brigit and the clothing that she wore. No, it can't be, this is absurd to even contemplate. If he had journeyed back in time, how far back could he have gone?

Sam closed his eyes to concentrate; there must be some reasonable explanation. He must have finally snapped. That must be it. Coming to Cornwall brought back too many memories of Danny and his other teammates. All that nonsense that his friend had been feeding him for so long must've finally emerged from his subconscious. It had to be some kind of illusion that his mind was creating for him. Sam's old physics professor would've had a perfectly logical and scientific explanation for what was happening to him. His professor would've said…Sam groaned as he opened his eyes and looked once again at Brigit. Sam knew what his professor would've said. He was very logical, but he also believed in the mysterious laws of nature. "Sam, anything in the universe is possible. There is an abundance of knowledge out there that we have yet to absorb or even begin to understand. Always keep an open mind."

"Sam, you look pale, are you ill?" Sam glanced around at the trees and up at the stars. He shook his head in response to Brigit's question. "No, I'm not ill, just a little lost."

It had been a restless night for Sam. His thoughts were in too much turmoil to make sense of anything. They decided to sleep in the meadow where the inn should've been. He didn't quite get his soft bed, but he wasn't complaining too loudly. At least with Brigit lying next to him, he was warm. He didn't say too much more to her last night after the realization sunk in that he might actually be somewhere, or should he say sometime, in the past. He was determined this morning to explore this further with Brigit.

Sam looked over at Brigit feeling her movements as she came awake. For a brief moment their eyes met. He was in awe of her beauty. Those eyes, he could easily drown in their blue depths. Her lips were sensuous and inviting. Sam fought the sudden urge to lean over and kiss her. What's the matter with me? I'm acting like a sixteen-year-old boy in hormonal overdrive. She's just a kid, but she makes me feel things no other woman ever has before.

As soon as Brigit realized that she was laying in Sam's arms, she sat up with a start. Her cheeks turned a rosy hue as she quickly pulled herself up and started to walk toward the path leading back to the stones. Sam stood up and grabbed his jacket and her cloak and followed. "Where are you going in such a hurry?" Sam wrapped her cloak around her and then put on his own jacket.

Brigit pointed straight ahead as she continued to walk. "I'm heading to the stream to bathe, and I would appreciate not having company while I'm doing so!"

An hour later, after taking turns bathing in the stream, Sam and Brigit were sharing a meager breakfast, consisting of some freshly picked berries and an apple that Sam had found in his jacket pocket. Brigit boiled water in the two cups that she had and made chamomile tea for the two of them to drink. Sam wrinkled his nose as he took a sip. "I'd rather have a strong cup of java but at least it's hot."

Brigit enjoyed the soothing brew as she sipped her tea. "What is java?"

Sam finished his tea and handed his empty cup back to her. "It's another word for coffee, a very necessary drink for many people, especially in the morning."

"We have to find more food today. This breakfast won't satisfy me for very long." Sam was picturing pancakes, eggs and sausage in his mind while he finished his last berry. Brigit nodded at him in understanding as she packed her cups away. "Maybe we can find a village today where we can barter for some bread and cheese."

Brigit fastened her cloak and gathered her possessions. She then stood up and turned to Sam. "We must be on our way now, if you are coming with me."

Sam was unsure about leaving the circle of stones. If he ventured too far, would he be able to find his way back to his own time again? "Where is it that we are going? I think we need to talk first. I have a lot of questions that I need to find answers to." He took Brigit's bundle and carried it for her as he walked beside her. "We can talk along the way Sam, but I think we should try and find you different clothing the first chance that we get. You appear quite odd dressed as you are, people will think you a lunatic!" Sam rolled his eyes heavenward. Considering where he was, they'd probably be right!

They walked a little ways without saying anything, each deep in their own thoughts. Sam was the first to break the silence. "Where is your home?"

Although Brigit was considered tall, she still had to look up to see Sam's face. His question had brought a tightness in her throat that made it hard to answer him. "I do not have a home, at least not anymore. My home was destroyed two months ago by soldiers of the king. My parents were murdered by those evil monsters, while trying to escape. I was away from the village at the time, gathering herbs for my mother in the forest. She was a healer and taught me much of her craft. That is how I have been bartering for food on my journey. I would help the ill in the villages that I came upon in exchange for some bread or a bed to sleep in for the night."

Sam felt a surge of anger renew itself within him as he listened to Brigit. He understood the pain she was feeling only too well. "I'm sorry to hear that Brigit. Do you not have any other family you can go to?"

Brigit shook her head as she tried to fight back the tears that threatened to fall. "I had a brother named Dunae, but he was lost to us many years ago. When King Arawn took over as ruler to our land, many of the young men of the villages tried to fight his soldiers in order to end their atrocities. Though he was only in his fourteenth year, Dunae went along to fight. My parents tried to stop him, but he was determined to go and fight for his people, the Pritani. That is who we are. We never saw him again. King Arawn's men destroy anyone who tries to stop them, including young boys…"

Sam stopped asking questions for the moment. He wanted to absorb all that Brigit was telling him. King Arawn reminded him of Randall Douglas. Both men used others to further their wealth and power, and did not care who died or suffered at their hands. History does have a way of repeating itself. Speaking of which, Sam was recalling a little of his high school history. He remembered studying the ancient Celtic civilization, though most of what he learned was lost somewhere in his subconscious. One word stuck out though, Pritani. Sam recalled that this was the name the Celts had called themselves at one time. Danny even talked about them too. Sam stopped all of a sudden in the middle of the field that they were crossing. Brigit looked questioningly at Sam while she waited for him to continue onward. Then she saw his face. He looked as if he were in a trance.

"What is the matter Sam, why did we stop?"

Sam sat down in the shade of a huge oak tree, pulling Brigit down next to him. "I was remembering something a friend told me once about the Pritani. They were an ancient culture that existed thousands of years ago from where, or I guess I should say when, I came from."

Brigit looked at Sam as if he'd lost his senses. Could it be that he really was a lunatic? "Sam, that is impossible. I am of the Pritani. Try as he might, King Arawn has not destroyed all of us yet. Many of us still do exist."

Sam took her hand and looked into her eyes. "You don't understand, Brigit. What I'm about to tell you may sound crazy. I don't believe it, though I know it must be true. Somehow, I have arrived here from the future. How, or why, is still a mystery to me, but for some reason fate has brought me here."

Sam was expecting Brigit to argue with him or even look frightened, as if he were utterly mad. She did neither of these. Instead she surprised him by smiling at him. Her eyes glowed as they reflected the morning sun, and he thought that maybe she didn't understand what he was telling her.

"I do not think you crazy, Sam. I believe that you have come from a far distance. After my parents were killed, I decided to make it my purpose in life to avenge their deaths. I prayed every night to the goddess Aerone to send me a mighty warrior to help me in my quest. She has answered my prayers and sent you to me, Sam. You will help me fight King Arawn and his men. You will help me bring victory to my people, so that they may once again live in peace."

The soldier in Sam was ready to fight, but the mercenary was asking what's in it for me? This is not my battle he thought. I've fought too many battles as it is and I'm too weary to fight anymore. Especially one that they couldn't possibly win, with just the two of them against an entire army. Even an ex-seal had his limits. He was about to explain this to Brigit when he made the mistake of looking once again into her eyes. Those damn eyes. They'll be the death of me yet! Truer words could not have been said if Sam was idiotic enough to agree to this, but he knew that he would. She would only continue on her own if he decided not to help her. Well, I guess this is as good a place or time to die as any other. "How do you plan on doing this, Brigit? I hope you have a plan, because I'd certainly like to hear it."

Brigit looked at Sam with such adoration that he hoped that he would be somewhat worthy of it. "There is a holy well about a half day's journey to the west. It is surrounded by an old monastery that is hidden in the forest. Many of the survivors from the battles with King Arawn's soldiers have gone there to live. They believe the waters from the well will heal them. Some of them are still able to fight, but they need someone to lead them. If we could go there and enlist the able ones, we may be able to win against King Arawn once and for all. The clerics who now reside at the monastery will surely assist us also, since a victory over King Arawn's rule would give them religious freedom once again. It was the clerics and their priest that brought law and order to my people, until the priest had taken ill. One of the clerics, who was called Arawn, took his place in his absence. The power was too much for Arawn, and soon his dark side emerged and he took over the land, acquiring an army of evil demons from the murderers that were kept in the dungeons. You can lead them Sam; I know you will succeed. Arawn does not feel the clerics or the wounded soldiers a threat. He will not expect another fight from any of them."

Sam listened carefully to Brigit as she spoke. Military tactics and maneuvers ran through his mind as he sat there and listened. If he could get enough worthy fighters and show them some moves, they may actually make it work. "Where is this King Arawn now? How do we find him?"

Brigit's heart swelled at Sam's words. He was going to help her. She must remember to thank Aerone in her prayers tonight. "He remains at the old monastery in Turoe, about a day's journey from where the clerics reside now. Using some of the villagers as slaves, he made it into a fortress, after having driven out the priest and his followers. He does not know of their new dwelling and some of the villagers who helped build the fortress escaped and are now at the holy well also. They may be able to tell you of the different ways to enter inside, so that we can take Arawn by surprise."

Sam pulled Brigit up with him as he stood up. "Well, I guess we better get started then..."

They walked a short distance before Brigit remembered something else to tell Sam. "I forgot to tell you Sam. The forest of the holy well is considered sacred by my people. To keep the sacred grounds safe, a wild boar is kept by the entrance of the forest, as a sort of protector, but that won't be any problem for you Sam. You are the mighty warrior sent by Aerone to fight wild boar and evil soldiers." She grabbed Sam's hand and pulled him along with her as they took a path leading westward. Sam just shook his head. Evil kings, ruthless soldiers and now a wild boar. Well, it could've been worse he thought, the way his luck had been running these past two days. She could've asked him to slay a fierce dragon for her. Looking at her glowing face as she led him along the path, he knew he would've too..."Wild boar huh...I wonder what that tastes like on the grill?" Sam's stomach growled a hearty response to that question.

The fire flickered bright in the great hall of the monastery. Sam and Brigit arrived there shortly before dark, and once Brigit explained their reason for being there, they were greeted with much enthusiasm. Sam and Brigit sat at a long wooden table with the clerics and the priest and some of the fallen warriors. They feasted upon fresh bread and wine, and, of course, the main entrée of wild boar. Brigit did not think that Sam intended to kill the animal but, considering that the wild beast was heading right for Sam, she understood why he did it. Though she didn't understand how. He pulled out something from beneath his arm and then suddenly there was a loud noise. The next thing she saw was the wild boar lying dead on the ground. She looked in wonder at Sam, knowing for certain that he must indeed be the great warrior Cu Chulainn. She helped Sam carry the animal to the monastery, apologizing for the fact that they had to slay the poor beast that protected their sacred woods. The clerics were at first angry, but calmed when Brigit told them of Sam's bravery and his reason for being there. They had prayed endlessly to the great goddesses of the Earth, hoping for an answer too. Here was a lovely maiden, graced with the name of one of their beloved goddesses, bringing a great warrior to them, albeit a strangely garbed one. Oh well, the powers that be did work in mysterious ways.

Sam was up early the next morning, after a good night's rest. He had been exhausted and slept like a rock in the bed that the priest provided for him. It was much more comfortable than sleeping on leaves, but it didn't have the same warmth that Brigit had provided for him. She had been given a room of her own, away from Sam and the soldiers.

Sam stood in the courtyard near the holy well with the other warriors. His denim jacket had been replaced by a knee length linen tunic that was trimmed in braided leather. He wore this over his black T-shirt. For his own modesty-sake and comfort, he kept his blue jeans on, refusing to part with them, despite Brigit's urgings to do so. After a brief inventory of what he had to work with, he was able to pick out five men who seemed capable to be trained to fight in the manner in which Sam was used to. Of course, there wouldn't be any M-16's or Mac 10's to assist them in their endeavor, but Sam was used to improvising. They would have to make do with the spears and bows and arrows and other weapons that the clerics helped them make. Sam showed them how to turn clay pots into bombs. He found some sulphur on the wall of a nearby cave and combined it with some saltpeter and charcoal that they had at the monastery. He poured this mixture into a cloth bag and stuffed it into a clay pot, with a piece of rope sticking out to be used as a fuse. Sam instructed the clerics to make as many more of these bombs that they could in the allotted time that he gave them. He worked day and night with the other men for five days. It was a condensed and somewhat varied version of the basic training he had gone through, but it would have to do. Sam felt alive again. He felt a bond taking form between the six of them. That's how it started with his old seal team…it was just the six of them. Sam was determined that this time there would be a better outcome for this team.

Sam didn't see much of Brigit during those five days, except during mealtimes when she would bring food out to them in the courtyard. She would watch them for a while, then go back inside and continue to help the clerics and other men in making their weapons. She had tried to get Sam to teach her his maneuvers also, determined to fight by his side with the others. Even though Sam was used to women in the military, he could not fathom having Brigit exposed to the dangers that they would be facing. He would never forgive himself if anything ever happened to her, so he refused her on the reasoning that his tactics were designed for only a six-man team. Brigit was disappointed, but did not argue further. Aerone had sent Sam to her, and she would not prove herself ungrateful.

On the evening of the fifth day, Sam sat in the hall by the fire with Brigit. They were alone for the first time in days. Everyone else had already retired for the night, eager to be on their way the next day to King Arawn's fort. Sam would be leaving early in the morning with the other five men. Brigit would not be going with them.

"Please, Sam, let me at least join you on this journey. I promise to stay away from the battle, but I want to be there when it is over. I know you will win Sam."

Sam looked at her as she sat beside him on the floor upon a large bearskin that lay in front of the hearth. Her hair shimmered in the firelight, and this time Sam did not resist the temptation to take some of the long silky strands and let them glide through his fingers. Sam had never felt this way about a woman before. He would forfeit his life to protect her. He would give up all his causes and build a home somewhere if he knew Brigit would be there too. Sam couldn't believe he was having these crazy thoughts, but he couldn't help it. Though he hadn't realized it at the time, or maybe just didn't want to, he had fallen for Brigit the moment she first looked at him with those incredible eyes. If he had to be stuck in the past, at least he had Brigit to share it with. Or did he? He did not know what fate the next few days would bring…or for that matter, if he would suddenly return to the future as quickly as he left it.

Sam moved his hand from Brigit's hair to her face and softly caressed her cheek. He tilted her chin up and leaned over to her, breathing in the flowery scent of her. His lips lightly touched hers at first, and with Brigit's encouragement, he deepened the kiss. He was overwhelmed by the feelings that she inspired in him. He had to stop soon, or he wouldn't be able to. He knew her to be young and still a virgin. There would be another time, but tonight wasn't it. If he did come back alive, he would ask her to share his life with him. Somehow, he knew, he would come back for Brigit. They lay there by the fire all night and slept in each other's arms. Just before dawn, Sam arose and left Brigit sleeping as he joined the other men setting out on their journey to King Arawn's fortress.

It was in the early hours of the next day that Sam and the other warriors made their way into the fortress. They had arrived late last night and slept hidden among some trees. While the other warriors slept, Sam moved stealthily around the fortress, scouting out just how many of the enemy they would be facing. He counted twenty warriors patrolling the walls, and guessed that there would be at least twice as many, if not more, inside. Two at a time, he carried over the clay bombs and placed them strategically around the high walls.

When the first light of dawn crept into the sky, the six men were ready to fight. They crept up to the walls of the fortress, the six of them hidden by the mists of the early morning. They each carried an unlit torch with them. Sam lit each one for them with matches that he carried in his jeans pocket. He then signaled for them to go to each spot where he had placed a bomb and ignite it. The explosions brought down half the men on the wall, the others were too stunned to fight back with too much enthusiasm, and they were swiftly taken care of with the spears and bows and arrows that the six man team carried. They proceeded inside, where most of the soldiers lay asleep and were caught off guard. They still fought hard, but the tactics that Sam taught his warriors gave them the advantage. None of King Arawn's warriors knew tae kwon do or any of the pressure points on the body that one can touch to incapacitate them long enough to finish them off. Sam told the others to leave Arawn for himself. He wanted the satisfaction of avenging Brigit's family, and in some way he felt he was avenging his seal team also. Though Arawn could be devious and slimy, Sam had an advantage over his evilness…a 9mm handgun. For once the good guys won.

Sam returned to the monastery where Brigit waited for him. They enjoyed a victory celebration in the great hall with all the men, along with the clerics and the priest. Once again peace would rule throughout the land.

After the celebration, Sam took Brigit by the hand and pulled her along with him into the courtyard by the holy well. They went for a walk in the moonlight, holding hands, making plans.

"Just how old are you, Brigit?"

Brigit enfolded herself into Sam's arms and sighed. "I am in my twentieth year, Sam, why do you ask?"

Sam gave a sigh of relief…."Oh, just curious…" At least she's of legal age, thought Sam. They continued to walk, until they came upon a circle of stones that stood on the other side of the courtyard. Sam never noticed them before. They were much smaller than the ones he had encountered at the dolmen, Boscawen-un. He stepped into the inner circle with Brigit and held her as they looked upon the stones.

Suddenly, the stones began to vibrate, and there was a loud humming coming from the circle. Sam pulled Brigit closer to him and held her tight within his embrace. He was afraid that he was being transported back to the future, but he didn't want to leave Brigit behind. Once again, visions of his seal team flashed in his mind. He could see them standing in front of him. He could hear himself yelling to them to go back. Another flash of light appeared, and then darkness.

Sam opened his eyes, afraid of what he'd find. Was he back in his own time? More importantly, was Brigit still with him? He sat up slowly and then looked around. It was difficult to see through the misted darkness. He stood up and called out Brigit's name. He heard a soft moan coming from behind one of the stones and ran over to it. He found Brigit standing there, leaning against the stone with her eyes closed. "Brigit, are you okay?"

Brigit opened her eyes and looked up at Sam. "Sam, what has happened? I feel so dizzy all of a sudden. The noise was deafening, and I heard you shouting at someone, and then I think I must have fainted."

Sam wasn't sure what had happened, he was just glad that Brigit was with him. "Let's go back to the courtyard, Brigit, and rest until our heads clear." They walked slowly back, both still a bit dizzy from the experience. They found the holy well, but everything looked different. There was no longer a courtyard, and there were just ruins where the monastery had stood only moments before.

Brigit looked startled. "Sam, everything is gone. Where is everyone?" Sam knew where everyone had gone. They had been gone for thousands of years now. Sam and Brigit had returned to the year 1999. At least Sam returned, for Brigit it would be a new journey.

"Well, Brigit, it looks like you're wearing odd clothes now, too. How would you like a pair of blue jeans of your very own?"

Brigit did not understand at first what Sam was talking about. She looked around at the ruins and then it came to her. She was in Sam's world now. She couldn't imagine what wonders awaited her, but, with Sam by her side, she was eager to discover them. A sadness came over her as she thought of her family that was lost to her, but now Sam would be her family.

Sam took Brigit's hand. "Shall we go, my lady? The new millenium awaits you." They found a path to follow and started on their way. After only walking a few feet, Sam heard a noise coming from behind one of the trees. He reached for his handgun and pulled Brigit behind him. A bright light suddenly appeared through the darkness. "What's the matter, Sammy…getting nervous in your old age?" Sam had truly thought nothing more could surprise him, until now. He stood motionless as the light moved closer to him and the man holding the flashlight came into view. "Sammy, you look like you've just seen a ghost. Quit fooling around, it's getting late; we should be getting back to the inn. Who's that with you?"

The lump that Sam felt in his throat made it difficult for him to speak. "Danny—how—where did you come from? They told me you were dead. They said I was the only survivor from the team when we got ambushed in North Africa."

Danny stood in front of Sam and looked into his eyes. "Do I look like a dead man? You seem to be confused, Sammy. If it hadn't been for your warning, you would've been the only survivor. You yelled for us to get back just before a string of claymore mines exploded. We got through that day and saved the hostages at the camp. How can you forget that Sammy? Are you feeling okay?"

Sam was confused. How could this be? Then he remembered that when he and Brigit were in the inner circle of the stones, he had dreamt that he was back in North Africa, five years ago. He saw his team advancing and yelled for them to go back. Could it be that he hadn't been dreaming after all? Had he really returned to that moment, and was able to warn his team of the ambush? Looking at Danny standing there in front of him, he knew it to be true. "Danny, I have a lot to tell you. You're not going to believe any of it."

Danny smiled at Sam's words. "Don't tell me you've had one of those mysterious experiences that people claim to have in the dolmens here in Cornwall. I had to practically twist your arm to come with me in the first place, because you thought it to be a bunch of old wives tales. You understand now, don't you Sammy?" Danny suddenly noticed that someone was standing behind Sam. "Who's that you got with you Sammy?"

Brigit came from behind Sam to meet Danny. She was about to introduce herself to him, thinking he looked familiar, when all of a sudden she let out a small cry. Sam quickly grabbed her back to him. "What's the matter Brigit? Are you alright?"

All of a sudden, Brigit broke loose from Sam's grasp and jumped into Danny's arms. A look of surprise on Danny's face soon changed to recognition and he closed his arms around Brigit and hugged her back. Sam was getting angry now. "What the hell are you doing Danny? Get your hands off her!"

Brigit let go of Danny and turned to Sam. "Sam, it's Dunae, my brother. He is much older now, but I would know him anywhere." Sam looked at Danny, and thought for sure now that he had lost his mind.

Danny started laughing at poor Sam. He really did look as if he was about to lose his mind. "My real name is Dunae, Sam. When I was fourteen, I found myself lost after watching all the other men from my village slaughtered. I don't even remember how I escaped. I followed a path through the forest and walked into a circle of stones. The stones began to vibrate, and the next thing I could remember was awakening and finding myself in an entirely different world. I was found by a retired professor, who had been studying the dolmens when he came upon me. He believed my story and took me with him back to the States, where I lived until I joined the military and met you, Sam. I didn't think I'd ever see any of my family again, until now." He looked at Brigit and once again held her tight in his arms.

Brigit looked at the two most important men in her life standing side by side. She took each one of their arms and folded them about her. She felt safe within the inner circle of their arms.

CROSSING THE BRIDGE

"What lies behind us and what lies before us
are tiny matters compared to what lies within us."

—Ralph Waldo Emerson

CHAPTER ONE

Do you ever close your eyes and just listen to the noise that the world seems to make all around you? When I was younger and living in my hometown of Koblenz, Germany, I would run and play with my friend Greta. When we finally wore ourselves out, we would fall down into the grass and lay there with our eyes closed. We could hear the birds talking to each other as they flew up into the clouds and the wind whooshing through the trees, and Greta's brother Friedrich chasing after the chickens that escaped from their shed. We could hear our own giggles as we shared whispered secrets and our hopes and dreams.

My favorite sounds came at night. Lying in bed, I could hear my Mutti humming as she washed the dishes; my Vater's voice resonating softly as he called out goodnight to me and told me he loved me; my cat Minka purring gently as she curled up against me in my bed. I felt loved and I felt safe. I would fall asleep feeling that everything was right in the world, at least in my world. After a few months, everything in my world would change.

When I was five, war started in our country. Vati told me that he would have to leave us for a while. When I asked him why, he said that he didn't know himself. He was told that he would have to serve his country, even though he didn't believe in the war they were fighting. After he left, I didn't like closing my eyes at night anymore. My mutti stopped humming. Vati's voice was not there to say goodnight to me. I still had my cat Minka, but her purring was no longer a comfort to me. It was replaced by the sounds of warplanes flying over our house.

There was no longer my friend Greta. Her family moved away right before my vater left. When I asked Mutti why, she said it was because Greta and her family were Jewish and Germany was a dangerous place for them to be right now. I didn't understand then. I don't think that I'll ever understand. Mutti said they went somewhere safe. I hope someday I can feel safe again, and be with my friend Greta.

CHAPTER TWO

The war brought many changes to our town. Except for the vegetables we grew in our garden and the milk and eggs we were able to buy from some of the farmers, food was scarce. We didn't have much money to buy new clothes, so Mutti would have to keep adjusting my dresses to fit me through my growing spurts. I hoped the war would end soon, because I continued to grow and Mutti was running out of dress material.

A couple of weeks before Christmas, our first Christmas without Vati being there, my mother cut some branches off a pine tree in our yard and brought them in for us to decorate. We would not be having a real tree this year, but Mutti tried to add a little cheer to our house. She draped them on the windowsills and we placed some of our Christmas balls on them. The smell of pine and the shiny balls cheered us.

Vati had been away for four months already, and we'd only received two letters from him. I guess it was hard for him to send us letters, since he was on a ship in the middle of the ocean. His ship was the 'Graf Spee'. Vati wrote that it was a German battle cruiser and, though he couldn't give us too many details on their mission, Mutti and I would listen to the war news and hear about Vati's ship. So far they had sunk nine British cargo ships, but not a single crewman or passenger on any of the sunken vessels were killed. I liked hearing that. I knew my vater would not like having to kill anyone, even during war.

A week before Christmas, we received notice that my vater was killed during an attack against his ship. My mutti didn't cry when she read the notice. Instead she just stared at my vater's picture hanging on the wall while she rocked me and wiped my tears for me. I heard her later that night, though. While I lay in my bed with my eyes closed, I heard Mutti crying as she sat in our living room. The same room from where Vati used to call out goodnight to me. I would never hear Vati's voice again. I wondered if I would ever hear Mutti humming again. Even Minka didn't purr anymore. The war was moving closer to our town, and the planes flying over our house would frighten her.

Soldiers came to Koblenz a few months later. Mutti said that they were Americans. They would go through each house, searching the rooms. When they came to our house, I hid with Minka under my bed. I could hear them talking to each other, but didn't understand the words they used. I just knew that they frightened me. As I lay under the bed, one of the soldiers came into my room. Minka ran out from under the bed at that moment, startling the American. I could see him raise his gun as he turned toward the bed, and I moved farther against the wall. He crouched down and looked under my bed, spotting me hiding there. His look of surprise turned into a smile when he saw me. He said something that I didn't understand, but he had kind eyes and suddenly I wasn't afraid anymore. He stood up and left along with the other soldiers. Mutti came into my room and helped me out from under the bed. That night I climbed into bed with her and we slept with Minka purring between us.

CHAPTER THREE

Days turned into months and the war still continued to move closer to our town. It had been two years since we lost my vater. It was hard for Mutti without him. She would act very brave, but I knew that she was scared of the war. We decided to go and stay with my Oma, who lived high up in the mountains. She was my vater's mutti, and missed him as much as we did. She lived alone and was more than glad to have us stay with her.

We packed only what we could carry on our backs in our rucksacks, along with a basket with food for the journey. I wanted to take Minka with us, but Mutti said that it would be too far for her to go and it would be too hard to carry her. We had to walk and it would take us all day. One of our neighbors was willing to take her. We left early in the morning, just before dawn.

We had been walking for several hours and I was getting very tired. I was too big for my Mutti to carry me and I wanted to stop and rest. I had insisted on carrying the basket and it was getting heavier every mile that we walked. Mutti said that we had to keep going if we were going to get to Oma's before dark. As we walked along the road, a truck carrying soldiers drove by. They pulled over to the side of the road and one of the soldiers jumped down to talk to us. They were the Americans and spoke the words that I didn't understand. Mutti could understand a little of what the soldier was saying. When he bent down to look at me, I recognized him as the soldier who had come into my room. He smiled at us and motioned for us to follow him to the truck. Then he held out his hand and helped Mutti and me up onto the back of it. The other soldiers moved over to make room for us. I think we were too tired to be scared, and happy for the ride. Mutti showed him on a map where we were going and the American nodded. During the ride, something started moving in the basket I had placed between my legs. The soldiers looked at it warily, but Mutti knew right away what it was, even before Minka stuck her head up through the basket cover. This caused a round of laughter from everyone on the truck, including my mutti.

We only had a short distance left to go after they dropped us off a few hours later. I wished that I knew what they were saying to each other, but I did understand when he told us his name was Harry Jamison. I told my mutti that I better learn their language if we're going to keep running into them.

We were planning on just staying with Oma for a few months, but word got to us that our town was almost completely destroyed by bombs, so we stayed for the duration of the war. Oma was glad to have us stay and we liked having someone to share memories of my vater. We felt safer so high up in the mountains.

Sometimes I would lie in the grass and stare at the clouds. They seemed so close that I would reach up with my arm and feel like I was actually touching them. I would think about my friend Greta and wondered where she was and if she ever thought of me. It had been four years since I last saw her. We both were only five years old. So much had happened in that time.

I had outgrown all of my clothes, so my Oma took some old dresses that my vater's sister had worn as a child and made them over for me. Oma is very good at sewing and she made them very pretty.

We were surprised to have the American soldier Harry Jamison come and visit us. Oma did not like him coming to her house. I think he liked my Mutti, and he would bring her flowers and chocolate bars for me. He would bring Oma presents too, like pretty soaps that smelled nice. She still did not like him coming over, but she finally let him come into the house. I think my Mutti started to like him too.

Harry helped me to learn some of his language, and Mutti and I would help him learn ours. He brought some picture books that he called 'comic books' with him when he came to visit. He would sit with me and point to the pictures and read the words to me slowly. After a few months, I was able to read the words to him. I don't think Oma liked it that Mutti and I were learning to speak English. She believed that the Americans were invading her homeland, and now her home. I think she was just afraid that Mutti and I would leave her to go to America, and that she would be lonely again.

It was in May of 1945 when Germany surrendered to the Americans and the war in our country was finally at an end. It had been six years since my vater died. I don't remember his face very well, but I still recall his voice in my dreams sometimes. Mutti gave me a locket that Vati had given her, and she put his picture in it so I could always look at it. We stayed with Oma until she passed away two months before the war ended. We decided to see what was left of our home in Koblenz. Harry drove us in a jeep and it reminded me of the last time we had traveled this road on our way to Oma's house. I didn't have Minka with me this time. She had lived a full cat's life in the mountains with us and Harry had dug a little grave for her in Oma's garden.

When we drove into our town, we were shocked by what we saw. Only a couple of buildings still stood. Our house was completely destroyed. Mutti's face turned white when she thought of what would've happened if we hadn't decided to leave when we did. We talked to one of our old neighbors, whose house was pretty much still intact. He told us that most of the people from the town got out in time before the bombs hit. He believed they'd be back again one day soon and start rebuilding the town. The ones that stayed behind were already sifting through the debris and salvaging what they could. It would take a long time, but Koblenz would one day thrive again.

A few months after the war ended, Mutti and Harry got married. Mutti had a new name now. It was strange at first hearing other people calling her 'Mrs. Jamison'. Harry wanted to adopt me and I told him that I'd like to think about it for a while. For the time being I still liked being called Marta Roesler.

CHAPTER FOUR

"Marta, wake up! The plane is landing."

I could hear Mutti's voice intruding in my dream as I slowly came awake. Opening my eyes, it took me a moment before remembering where I was. We were on a plane, descending to our new home with Harry. Flying in a plane had been exciting, but now a knot began forming in my stomach. I could see out the window that we were getting closer to the ground. Soon, I would be starting a new life in a country that was strange to me. Harry must've realized this. Reaching across my mutti, he took my hand and gently squeezed it. He smiled at me with those brown eyes that always showed so much kindness.

"I know it's seems a lot to take in all at once, Marta. I love you and your mom very much and I promise that I'll do whatever it takes to make you both happy here."

"You already make us happy, Harry, right Marta?"

Marta looked over at Harry and winked as she answered. "Right, *Mom*!"

*   *   *   *

"Why is this line so long, Harry?"

They were surrounded by people with suitcases piled everywhere. Harry nudged all their suitcases forward another inch as the line progressed slowly through airport customs.

"It's just one of those things you have to do when you come to a new country. The line seems to be moving now so it shouldn't be much longer. Then we'll get a ride from someone at the base. I'm still in the army for another two weeks, so we'll be staying at Fort Hamilton for the duration. That'll give us time to get through all the paperwork and find an apartment."

The next two weeks went by quickly. There were guest barracks for soldiers with families, and that's where we stayed with Harry. He said it's not the 'Ritz', which he explained was the name of a fancy hotel, "but we've got a great view of the harbor". From what I'd seen so far of New York City, I liked it. It was a lot bigger than Koblenz and there were a lot more people, but I found it fascinating.

Harry's brother came to the base to drive us around so Harry and *Mom* could look at apartments. He told me to call him Uncle Joey. He wasn't as tall as Harry, but he had the same brown eyes and blond hair. Mom and I have blue eyes but our hair is also blond, so we all looked like we really were from the same family. I pointed this out to Harry and Uncle Joey. Harry's smile faded as he looked over at me in the back seat of the car.

"Marta, honey, it wouldn't matter if you had blue hair with polka dots. We became a family when I married your mom, whether we look alike or not. You're my daughter now, and I hope you can come to think of me as your dad. And not only do you have me, but you've got an Uncle Joey, an Aunt Sheila and an Aunt Louise along with new grand-parents and a slew of cousins."

I sat there looking out the window at the passing buildings thinking about what Harry had just said. I didn't know if I was ready to have a new father yet. I just thought of Harry as my friend. He was a very nice man and was so good to my mom and me.

"Harry, do you think my new family will like me?"

Harry turned toward me, his smile returning.

"They won't be able to help themselves. Just ask your Uncle Joey."

Joey looked back at me through the mirror in the front of the car.

"That's right Marty girl, they'd be daft not to like you and your mom."

Their words made me feel better and the tightness that seemed to reoccur in my stomach lately seemed to lessen. I was no longer afraid to face the new life ahead of me, and I would never forget the life I left behind. We drove across a huge bridge. The river below glistened from the sunlight and a cool breeze wafted into the car through the open windows, which felt refreshing on such a hot summer day. There were people walking along a lane that was sectioned off from the main traffic. I saw mothers pushing strollers, older children following behind laughing and skipping, some of them stopping to watch the boats in the water.

"What do you call this bridge, Harry?"

"It's called the Brooklyn Bridge, Marta, and we're taking it to my old neighborhood where I grew up and where my family still lives. It's where I want you to grow up too. Brooklyn is a great place to live."

As we left the bridge and turned on to a wide street, Harry pointed out various places to us. It was such a difference from the ruins my mom and I left behind in Koblenz. Even before it was destroyed, our house was much smaller than the ones we were seeing now. Harry seemed so excited to be back in his 'old neighborhood', as he put it.

"That's Mrs. Rossilini's bakery over there, Marta. You can smell her bread baking in the morning over three blocks away. Here, on the corner where we're turning, is the church my family belongs to. Gee, I never thought to ask what church you go to, Anna."

Harry looked worried as he turned to face my mom.

She smiled back at him and then looked out the window as we drove by the church.

"It's a beautiful church Harry. I'm sure it'll be just fine for all of us."

Harry seemed relieved.

"I thought maybe someday, when we're settled in we could have a church wedding there. It would be a lot better than the civil service one we had in Germany. It's up to you if you want to, but it would be nice to have everyone there and…."

Harry stopped talking as mom leaned over and kissed him lightly on the lips.

"Yes Harry, it would be very nice."

Uncle Joey caught my eye as he glanced into his mirror, and we both made funny faces at each other and then laughed.

"Okay Harry, enough with the lovey dovey romance stuff. We're here."

Joey parked the car in front of what looked like a bunch of attached houses. Uncle Joey described them as brownstone apartments.

"Our parents live in those apartments across the street. Down the block lives our sister Sheila with her husband Tommy. They have three kids, Tommy Jr., who's four, Janie who's eight and Mary is, I believe, close to your age Marti, you're about twelve aren't ya?"

I nodded as I tried to take in all that Uncle Joey was saying to us.

"Then there's our sister Louise who still lives at home and is going to college, in Manhattan, mind you. A Brooklyn school wasn't good enough for her. She wants to be a journalist and get a Pulitzer or something someday."

Harry shook his head as he held the car door open for mom and me as we got out of the car.

"Okay Joey, that's enough. There's nothing wrong with Louise going to college somewhere outside of Brooklyn. There is more to the world than just our neighborhood in Brooklyn Heights. Let her explore it. Now if you don't mind, we've got an apartment to look for and some family to introduce."

Joey took my arm and led me across the street.

"Let's start with the introductions first. Knowing Ma, she'll have the scoop on anything available to rent in this area, and probably all of Brooklyn."

We walked up to a set of steps leading up to the building.

"This here is called a front stoop, and we like to sit on these steps at night, especially in the summer, to cool off and watch people go by."

We climbed the steps and Uncle Joey opened the front door, leading into a hallway. He led me down the hall to another door, which he opened, and we walked into a living-room. There was a large brown sofa and two matching chairs surrounding a low wooden table. In a corner, near a window, sat a woman in a rocking chair doing some sewing.

"Here they are Mom. Harry returned from the war safe and sound with a new family to boot."

I knew this was Harry's mom before Uncle Joey even said anything. She had the same brown eyes and blonde hair, though hers was streaked with gray. She wore a blue cotton print dress over her somewhat large frame. She looked quite stern as she answered her son.

"I am not so old yet that I can't see that for myself Joseph. It's too bad you were only in high school when your brother went off to war, or I would've made them take you too. Now go sit over there and be quiet."

Being duly chastised, Joey slumped down into one of the chairs, crossing his arms in front of him as he hung his legs over the armrest.

"Sit up straight Joseph, or better yet, make yourself useful and go get that wife of yours from upstairs and bring her down here to meet Harry and the others."

Joey got up and walked over to the door. He turned to look at Harry before opening it.

"I wrote you about Helen, didn't I Harry? You missed our wedding two years ago."

Harry chuckled at Joey as he was about to leave.

"I guess my invitation got lost in the mail somewhere over Germany. You're lucky Hitler himself didn't show up instead. By the way Joey, you missed my wedding too."

After Uncle Joey left, the room seemed a lot quieter. He seemed to bring a room to life whenever he was in it. It was like he carried a lot of energy with him and it spilled over onto anyone who came near him. I really liked him. I heard the rocking chair creak and turned to see Harry's mom rising from it and coming over to where my mom and I were standing. There was that familiar tightness again as she approached the two of us. Suddenly her face broke out into a smile. A familiar smile, just like Harry's, as she held out her arms to my mom and me. I was surprised by this sudden change in her as I moved closer to her so she could hug me, and then my mother. I think Harry noticed my confusion. After his mom let me go, he led me over to the sofa and whispered in my ear.

"Her bark is always worse than her bite, Marta. She pretends to be mad at Joey but she adores him, and I had no doubt that she would welcome you and your mom into the family."

I settled down into the sofa next to Harry and leaned into him. "You have a great family, Harry." I looked up at him and smiled, the tension once again fading away. "We have a great family, Harry."

Harry put his arm around me and gently squeezed my shoulder as Uncle Joey returned with his wife.

She stood out among all of us blondes with her dark brunette hair. She had blue eyes that smiled when they looked over at Harry, but turned colder as she looked over at me and my mom, who now sat down beside us on the sofa.

"Here she is Harry. This is Helen, the love of my life and the future mother of my soon to be son."

This he said as he patted Helen's very round belly.

"Oh, stop it, Joey. I may decide to have a girl just to spite you."

Harry stood up to hug Helen and shake Uncle Joey's hand.

"Nice to finally meet the woman who would take pity on my brother and marry him. Congratulations! When's the baby due?"

Helen moved over to one of the chairs as Uncle Joey helped her sit down.

"Not soon enough for me. I still have two months to go. The doctor says around the end of September."

The smile she gave Harry faded as she looked at mom and me. No one else seemed to notice as I looked around the room. She politely nodded as Harry introduced us to her, then Mom got up to help Harry's mom make coffee and refreshments in the kitchen. Uncle Joey sat down on the armrest next to Helen looking down at her with those same 'lovey dovey' eyes he teased Harry about earlier in the car.

Harry and Uncle Joey visited while they waited for the coffee to be done.

"So, Joey, where is our dad on a Saturday morning? I was sure he'd be here to meet Anna and Marta."

Before Uncle Joey could answer, Harry's mom stood at the entrance to the kitchen and answered for him.

"He's at the docks, of course. Where you'll always find him every spare minute. Being one of the foremen, he thinks he has to always be there whenever a new shipment comes in, even on his day off. Oh well, it keeps him out of my hair. You should work Saturdays too, Joey, and keep out of Helen's hair."

"Helen likes it just fine that I work only Mondays through Fridays at the docks, Ma. Especially with the baby coming and all. Besides, we have to leave some work for Harry, too, now that he's back from Germany, and will probably want his old job back. Right Harry?"

Harry got up and pulled me along with him as his mom motioned for us to follow her into the dining room, where the coffee was being served.

"That's okay Joey, someone else can have it. I took a test a couple of weeks ago for a government job. Starting next month, I'm going to be working at the post office here in Brooklyn Heights. I sure lucked out on that one. I could've wound up somewhere in Manhattan or Queens."

Uncle Joey shuddered as we entered the dining room. "Manhattan or Queens?…Don't even joke about it brother! Ya gotta stay on this side of the bridge."

CHAPTER FIVE

The summer passed quickly for us. Harry's mom, who asked me to call her grandma, told us about an apartment that her friend Mrs. Jacobs had available to rent in her building only three blocks away. Mrs. Jacobs has known Harry since he was a boy, and was glad to let us have the apartment. It felt good to finally leave the army base and settle into our new home.

Harry's parents gave us some extra furniture that they had in their basement, so I sleep now in Aunt Louise's old bed from when she was a kid. The first night that we stayed in our new place, I went to bed early after a long day of moving and unpacking. I closed my eyes and as I was drifting off to sleep I could hear my mom in the kitchen humming while she put away her dishes, and Harry in the living room as he called out good-night to me.

After a few weeks, we finally had everything unpacked and put away and became familiar with our new neighborhood. Mom and I would walk to the corner grocer, which was owned by Mr. Nichols, and buy milk and eggs and whatever we needed for supper. Harry started his job at the Post Office and would be gone all day, so Mom and I would find things to do. Harry told me that school would be starting in a couple of weeks and continued to help me with my English after supper each night.

Each Sunday, after church, we go to Harry's parents' home for dinner. Grandpa then asks me to read the Sunday funnies out loud to him so that I can practice my English. We take turns reading them, and Grandpa makes us all laugh when he changes his voice as he reads the different comics. My favorite is "Steve Canyon," the pilot who flies around the world, meeting up with different villains, including the beautiful 'Copper Calhoun'. Grandpa says he doesn't go for all that 'military intrigue'…"Give me 'Little Orphan Annie' instead. At least I can relate to Daddy Warbucks, neither one of us has hair."

Today Mom and I went shopping for school supplies. I got two new dresses and a pair of shoes, and some notebooks and pencils. As we returned home, we came upon Mrs. Jacobs sitting on the front stoop.

"Looks like you two have been doing some shopping. Did you find something nice at Loehman's?"

I opened the packages and showed her what we bought.

"Those dresses will look real pretty on you, Marta. I bet you can't wait until school starts next week. You'll finally get to meet kids your own age."

Mom took my bags as I sat down next to Mrs. Jacobs on the step.

"I'm going upstairs to start dinner, Marta. You can stay and visit for awhile."

"Okay Mom, I'll be up soon."

After my mom shut the door behind her, I sat there thinking about school. I forgot that Mrs. Jacobs was even there until she started talking and startled me out of my thoughts.

"Well, Marta, are you just going to stare at the sidewalk or are you going to say something?"

"I'm sorry Mrs. Jacobs, I guess my mind was on other things."

"Other things being school, and what the other children will think of you?"

I looked up at her. It was like she read my mind. She took off her glasses and brushed some of her gray hair out of her face. Then she took a handkerchief and wiped her forehead.

"Ayy, this heat…autumn won't come too soon for me." She put her glasses back on and looked over at me.

"Don't look so shocked. It doesn't take a genius to figure out that you would have some apprehensions about starting school in a new country and making new friends."

I looked down by my feet and watched some ants go into a crack on the step. "That's just it, Mrs. Jacobs, will I make new friends? Harry and his family have been so nice, and you're really great yourself, but I guess I wonder if the other kids will like me."

Marta wanted to say more but didn't know if she should. She made up her mind then and looked up at Mrs. Jacobs.

"You know my Uncle Joey's wife, Helen, don't you?" She continued when Mrs. Jacobs nodded. "Maybe it's just me, I don't think anyone else has noticed, but I don't think she likes Mom or me. Whenever she looks at us, she stops smiling and she doesn't talk to us unless we ask her a question, and then her answers are very curt. Why doesn't she like us, when she doesn't even know us? I guess I shouldn't be asking you, but I don't want to ask mom or Harry and get them upset."

Mrs. Jacobs put her hand on my shoulder.

"No, no…that's okay. I think I know the answer dear. I've known Helen since she was a little girl. I guess at my age, I've known everyone in this neighborhood since they were little. She was such a sweet little thing, with her pigtails and freckles. She followed her older brother everywhere, always trying to get into the games with him and his friends. Most big brothers would probably tell her to bug off and leave them alone, but not Jimmy. He adored his little sister and would let her stay and sit on the side to watch them play ball, and sometimes he'd let her join in. They were real close. Well, Jimmy went in the army about the same time as Harry did, and he was sent overseas too. Jimmy wasn't as lucky as Harry, though, and he didn't come back. Helen was devastated. I was glad she had Joey already by then to help her through it. I don't think Helen really blames you or your mom for what happened to Jimmy, but you probably remind her of it. Once she comes to terms with her grief, she'll respond better to you and your mom. Just give her time. Helen has a good heart, but right now it's a bit bruised."

I could see Harry at the end of the block, walking this way, so I got up and turned to Mrs. Jacobs.

"I guess I should be going up now. Harry's home and we'll be eating soon."

I climbed the steps and reached for the door handle. Before turning it, I looked down at Mrs. Jacobs again. She was staring out at the street, looking as lost in thought as I must've been a few minutes earlier. She was a nice lady, and I hoped that there was no one that she had lost in the war. Too many of us already had. I thought of my vater, and then heard Harry come up behind me. He greeted Mrs. Jacobs and then followed me inside.

"How's it going, squirt?"

I took his hand as we walked down the hall. "Everything's going great, *Dad*!"

*   *   *   *

Saturday I woke up to the wonderful aroma of baking bread. I jumped out of bed and ran into the kitchen. Mom and Harry were having coffee at the small kitchen table. I looked at the oven, but it was not on. Harry saw what I was doing and started to laugh.

"I told you that you can smell Mrs. Rossilini's bakery from three blocks away."

He must've noticed my disappointment because he got up and grabbed a box off the counter.

"Come on and sit down. I got these fresh from the bakery this morning. The best hard rolls you'll ever eat. Just slabber some of that butter and marmalade on it and you'll swear you're in heaven."

I took one of the rolls from the box and did what Harry said to do. He watched me as I took my first bite and then smiled as he saw my face light up.

"Dad, these are great. Mom, you have to try one too."

Harry set the box on the table and we all enjoyed our heavenly breakfast.

After breakfast I helped Mom clear off the table. She winked at Harry as she told me to go and get dressed because we were going someplace special today.

"Should I put on one of my new dresses?"

Mom shook her head as she unplugged the coffee pot. "Put on those dungarees that I bought you last month."

We took the F train to wherever we were going. I love riding the subway. I remember the first time Harry told me we were going to take a ride on the "subway". I misunderstood it for the word "submarine" in English. I pictured us going down under the water. I was very pleased to see that it was a train that we were going on instead.

As we got off the train and climbed the steps from the station, I could smell the ocean. When we got outside, I could see a huge roller coaster in the distance.

"Dad, what is this place?"

Harry grabbed my hand and pulled me along with him and my mom.

"This here, Marta, is Coney Island, and that great air that you're breathing in is from the Atlantic Ocean. Your mom and I figured, since school starts on Monday, we should have a fun family outing today. Now, what would you like to do first, eat one of their famous 'Coney' dogs or ride the Cyclone, that huge roller coaster over there?"

My mom looked at the roller coaster and then at Harry and me.

"I think, if I can make a suggestion, it would be wiser to go on the ride first, and then eat the hot dog. I will be waiting for you right over there."

Harry took mom's hand and pulled her with us.

"Oh no you don't, darling. You are going with us on that roller coaster. I do agree, though, with waiting until after we go on some of the rides before we eat."

It was a wonderful day. We rode the Cyclone three times. Well, at least Harry and I did. Mom wouldn't go on anymore after the first time. She did come on the Ferris Wheel with us, thinking it would be pretty tame after the roller coaster. Little did she know it wasn't called the "Wonder Wheel" for nothing. We all sat together in one of the cars, which rocked us back and forth as we moved to the top. The car then flew down a metal track and swung to a stop, and then it started rocking us again as we went around the wheel. I felt dizzy by the time the ride was over, but it felt good.

The hot dogs were delicious, and so were the ice cream cones we enjoyed as we walked along the boardwalk and watched the waves rolling onto the shore. I took my shoes off and walked bare-foot in the sand until it got too hot for me. Then I ran into the water to cool them off while Harry and Mom sat on some chairs and watched me.

The sun shone bright and the cool breeze coming off the Atlantic Ocean felt good. There was so much to see; I didn't know what to do next. That is, until I saw the tower up ahead.

"Dad, what's that over there?"

Harry looked up at where I was pointing.

"That's the Parachute Tower. They moved it over to the Steeplechase Park here at Coney Island a few years ago from the 1939 World's Fair. They lift you up 262 feet in the air with a parachute and then they drop you. Would you like to try it?"

Before I could say anything, Mom answered for me. "There's no way I'm letting either of you be dropped from up there, parachute or not!"

Harry winked at me as he put his arm around my mom and hugged her.

"Whenever you kiss me honey, I'm always flying without a parachute...but I agree that maybe we should wait until another time before we try that ride."

As the light started to fade, and evening crept up on us, we took a last walk along the boardwalk before heading home. We were exhausted as we headed back on the train. I had never had so much fun in my entire life.

"Coney Island is a fantastic place, Dad. Can we go again someday?"

Harry put his arms around Mom and me and hugged us to him. "We sure can, Marta, and next time we'll get your mom to go at least twice on the Cyclone."

After such an eventful Saturday, it was hard getting out of bed the next morning for church. Mom made sure that we did, though. Somehow I managed to stay awake during the sermon, my mind drifting to all the things we did the day before. After the service, we walked over to Harry's parents' home for our usual Sunday dinner.

Sunday afternoons, along with Harry's parents, usually consisted of Harry, Mom and me, and Aunt Louise. Sometimes Uncle Joey and Aunt Helen would join us, when they weren't eating with Helen's family. Today, Harry's sister Sheila and her family were included in the event. I'd never met them yet because they were away for the past month on vacation. Sheila's husband was a doctor and each summer he takes a month off from his practice and the whole family goes to some resort place in the mountains called the Poconos.

Aunt Sheila has red hair, though I don't believe that it is her natural color. Her eyebrows were too dark. It looked as if Aunt Sheila hadn't been born with the same blonde hair as her siblings. She must've inherited her dad's coloring. Harry said that his dad used to have brown hair before he lost most of it.

Tommy Jr. sat on the floor playing with his toy fire engine. Janie sat by her dad, brushing the hair of her doll she had on her lap. Mary, who was my age, sat by her mother, looking bored. When Grandpa told me to go and get the funny papers, I suddenly felt self-conscious about reading in front of the other children. I handed them over without reading any of the comics out loud to him.

"I guess you want me to go first this week, huh? Okay, let's see what Daddy Warbucks is up to today."

Grandpa read aloud while the others in the room listened. Grandma and Mom were in the kitchen and Aunt Sheila got up and joined them. I noticed that Tommy Jr. stopped playing with his toy while he listened to his grandpa read. Janie continued to play with her doll, but she giggled as grandpa changed his voice. Uncle Tommy ignored us as he read the business section of the newspaper. Harry and Aunt Louise were sitting together on the sofa looking at an old photo album. As I glanced around the room, I caught Mary's eye. She was staring at me with a smirk and I suddenly had the desire to leave the room. I decided to go and join my mother in the kitchen. Before I could leave, Grandpa had finished and beckoned me over.

"Come on now sweetheart, it's your turn."

I grabbed the paper back and opened it up. As I read aloud, I could hear Mary snickering. Harry noticed it too.

"That's really good Marta, honey. You're pronunciations are better than mine. You'll do just fine in school tomorrow, won't she, Mary?"

Mary looked over at Harry and nodded.

"Yes Uncle Harry, I'm sure she will." Mary got up and walked toward the kitchen. Just before she left the room, she added…"Especially if we have classes with Donald Duck or Mickey Mouse."

CHAPTER SIX

Monday morning, I woke up early. I didn't sleep very well the night before, but I attributed that to the normal 'first day of school' jitters. I wasn't going to let what Mary said bother me. Harry was angry at what she said and wanted to talk to her. I didn't want any tension between Harry and Aunt Sheila, so I told him it was okay. He started to argue with me but then Mom came into the living room to tell us dinner was being served. The rest of the afternoon was uneventful, and I found that Tommy Jr. and Janie were very different from their older sister and we had a good time playing a game together.

Mom was just scooping oatmeal into a bowl for me as I walked into the kitchen. "I want you to have a nourishing breakfast before you leave for school. Come, sit down while I pour you some milk. How are you doing, are you feeling nervous?"

I sat down and dipped my spoon in the sugar bowl and began to sprinkle it on my cereal.

"I'm a little nervous, Mom, but it's always like that on the first day of school, no matter what country you're from. Don't worry, I'll be okay."

I was just finishing my breakfast when Harry came into the kitchen.

"Are ya ready, Squirt? I'll walk with you to school on my way to work."

I stood up and grabbed my new schoolbag off the counter. Mom put her arm around me and kissed my cheek.

"You have a good day, Marta. I will see you this afternoon. It's going to be lonely around here with both you and Harry gone."

It was sunny out and the days were starting to cool down. Autumn would be starting in another two weeks. I felt a chill and buttoned my sweater as I walked beside Harry. He wasn't his usual jolly self and I was pretty sure it was because of me.

"Don't worry, Dad, I know I'm going to like school here in Brooklyn. I've always liked studying, and it may take me a little longer to grasp things until I'm more fluent with your language, but I can do it. If mom and I could survive bombs flying over our house during the war, I can handle my cousin Mary, though she could probably be just as explosive."

Harry laughed and hugged me and kissed the top of my head.

"You're right. You and your mom are both amazing. I knew it from the first moment I met both of you. Well, here's your school."

We stopped in front of a large brick building that was surrounded by a chain-link fence.

"You have a good day, Squirt. I'll see you at home later."

"Okay, Dad. You have a good day too."

Before Harry could turn away, I put my arms around his neck to hug him and whispered in his ear.

"I love you, Dad."

Then I let go and ran into the schoolyard. I didn't turn around to see if Harry was still standing there, even though I had a feeling that he was, and that he was smiling.

The schoolyard was filled with children of all ages and sizes. The younger children were playing on the swings and the teeter-totters, while the older ones stood around talking, some of the boys playing catch. I saw my cousin Janie skipping rope with some of her friends. She waved to me when she saw me. I smiled and waved back as I continued to walk closer to the school. I knew the bell would be ringing in a few minutes, so I decided to wait near the entrance. When I passed a group of girls that were standing near the fence talking, I could hear one of them snickering. It was a very familiar snicker. I looked up and saw Mary with her friends. She said something to them and then they all turned to look at me. I forced a smile and waved at Mary, but they all turned away and just ignored me. So much for first impressions.

The bell sounded and I followed everyone inside. I went to the office to find out where my class would be. Mrs. Linder, the secretary, told me that my sixth grade teacher would be Miss Hepner, and gave me directions to the classroom. The halls were filled with children finding their way to their classes and I went with the flow. I found room 409 and almost collided with Mary as she pushed ahead of me and went into the room. There are four sixth grade teachers at the Brooklyn Heights grade school, and that meant I had a one out of four chance of being in Mary's class. I guess the odds were against me that day.

Miss Hepner was standing behind her desk at the front of the classroom as I walked in. She was tall and thin and wore her black hair in a tight bun at the top of her head. She had on glasses that were attached by a chain around her neck. I could hear a nasal quality in her voice as she called out the attendance and assigned seats alphabetically.

Harry had registered me as Marta Jamison even though my last name is legally Roesler. I had finally agreed to let him adopt me, but it would still take a few months before it was finalized. When Miss Hepner called out my name, I sat down in the seat that she pointed to. That meant that I would be ahead of Mary, because Jamison came before Madison, which was her last name. I laid my schoolbag on my desk but before I could open it, out of the corner of my eye I could see Mary raising her hand. Miss Hepner looked annoyed to be interrupted.

"Yes, Miss Madison is it? Just be patient, I have a few names ahead of you still."

"But Miss Hepner, you have Marta in the wrong seat. She should be farther back in the class. Her last name starts with 'R'."

I could tell that Miss Hepner didn't like being told that she was wrong.

"What are you talking about young lady? Since when does the name Jamison start with an 'R', and what does this have to do with you?"

Mary looked over at me as she answered the teacher.

"Her last name isn't Jamison, it's Roesler. My Uncle married her mother, and she still has her father's last name. My mother told me so."

Miss Hepner walked over to my desk and looked down at me.

"Is that true Marta? We have to have your legal name for our records. If you have your father's last name, you must use it here. So now, what is your last name again?"

"Her last name is Jamison. I know because I'm her father and she has my name."

Miss Hepner was surprised to see a man standing at the doorway answering the question that she had posed to me. But not as surprised as I was, or Mary for that matter, if her mouth hanging open was any indication. Harry stood there scowling at my teacher. He looked over at me and smiled as he walked over to my desk.

"You forgot your lunch, Marta. I took it from you while you buttoned your sweater and halfway to work, I realized I was still holding it. You see I know it's yours, because it's got your name on it, Marta Jamison."

He looked over at Miss Hepner. "J-a-m-i-s-o-n, you got that?"

Miss Hepner nodded as she backed up to stand at her desk once again.

Harry turned toward Mary. "How about you?"

Mary swallowed a gulp as she nodded at her uncle. The rest of the class was enjoying this immensely. Anything to delay having to do class work was always preferable. Miss Hepner did not look like she was enjoying it.

"Enough of these interruptions. Miss Madison, please take your seat at the back of Miss Jamison's row."

Satisfied, Harry handed me my lunch and walked to the door. He turned and waved at me before he left. Miss Hepner didn't look too pleased with me. Not a very good start for the first day of school. Oh well, at least she has no doubt about my name anymore. Neither do I. I guess I can thank Mary for that.

The rest of the day was uneventful. Mary sat with her friends at lunchtime and decided to ignore me. It didn't hurt my feelings any. She and her friends seemed to fit well together. Unfortunately, no one else sat near me either. I don't know whether it's because they don't like me or they're afraid of going against Mary.

Walking home, I spotted Mom and Mrs. Jacobs sitting on the front stoop. I ran the rest of the way until I reached them.

"So, Marta, how was it?"

"It was okay, Mom. I don't think I'll be the teacher's pet any time soon, and I have Mary in my class, but otherwise it's fine. You should've seen what Dad did!"

I told her and Mrs. Jacobs about what Mary did and how Harry saved the day. Mrs. Jacobs laughed as I described Mary's face when Harry walked in.

"Maybe she'll mind her own business for once and stop being Miss knows-it-all. That Harry, he's one of the good ones. You and your mom are lucky to have him and he's lucky too. You three make a nice family. Well, I have to go in before the cake I have in the oven burns. I'll see you later."

We said goodbye to Mrs. Jacobs as she went inside. I sat down next to mom.

"So, do you have a lot of homework?"

I plopped my schoolbag on the ground by my feet and pulled out some books.

"Not too much. Just a couple of chapters to read in the science book, and some math in this workbook. I'll get it done after supper."

Mom got up and shook out her skirt.

"Why don't you go say hi to your grandmother then? I'm sure she'd like to hear about your school day. I'm going up to get the roast in awhile. You can come up and help me with the potatoes in about an hour."

"Okay, Mom."

I walked the short distance to where my grandparents lived, and went inside. As I followed the hall to their apartment, I heard thumping noises coming from upstairs. Curiosity getting the better of me, I climbed the stairs up to the second floor, where Helen and Joey lived. I was about to knock on their door to see if the noise was coming from there, when I heard it once again coming from above me. I knew the next set of stairs led to the roof, like it did in our building. The thumping started again so I decided to check it out. As I moved nearer to the roof door, I realized that the thumping was someone pounding on the other side of the door. Someone must've locked the door; not realizing anyone was up there. I unbolted the lock and opened the door. Staring at me from the other side was a boy about my age, leaning on crutches, a look of relief lit up his face.

CHAPTER SEVEN

"Hello there. What are you doing up here on the roof? Someone must've locked the door after you came up."

He moved aside to let me through and I came out onto the roof area. I'd never been on the roof before, even on our building. There was a low brick wall surrounding the roof, so that I was able to walk out and look over to the street below without fear of falling off. Looking across the tops of the buildings, I could see the Brooklyn Bridge. I turned back toward the boy standing there by the door watching me.

"This is great! You can see so much from up here. I've never seen the whole bridge before."

Leaning on his crutches, he walked over to stand next to me.

"You should see it at night, the stars look so close that you feel like all you have to do is reach up and you can touch them."

"That's what it felt like at my Oma's when we lived with her during the war. She lived up in the mountains."

"This Oma, is that your grandmother?"

Someone had brought up some lawn chairs and left them up here. I motioned for the boy to follow me and we both sat down.

"It's the word we use for grandmother in Germany, where I'm from. She passed away just before the war ended, but now I have a new grandmother. She lives downstairs on the first floor of this building. My Uncle Joey and his wife live here also, on the second floor."

"I know Joey. He's my friend. He comes up here with me sometimes at night. My mother doesn't want me to come up here by myself, so Joey comes with me and we look at the bridge all lit up at night. It looks really neat!"

He leaned his crutches against the wall next to us and it was then that I noticed the braces on his legs. He saw what I was looking at.

"I need them to help me walk. I had polio two years ago and it weakened my leg muscles. Most of the time my mom tries to keep me in my wheelchair. She thinks I'm going to fall off my crutches and hurt myself. I know she's just worrying about me but I can't seem to convince her that I prefer to fall once and awhile to always being in the chair. She works part-time at the beauty parlor around the corner. She goes there every afternoon during the week for a couple of hours, and that's my chance to get out of my wheelchair for awhile and come up here."

"It must be very difficult climbing the stairs with your crutches. What floor do you live on?"

"My mom and I live just down the hall from your uncle. It's just the one set of steps that I have to climb. It takes me awhile. I toss the crutches up ahead of me and then pull myself up holding on to the stair railings."

We sat in silence for a few minutes watching the birds playing on the roof. They were diving in and out of little water puddles that were left from the rain we had the night before. I could understand why the boy liked coming up here. I was the first one to speak again.

"My name is Marta. What's yours?

"I'm Michael."

We both extended our arms and shook hands.

"It's very nice to meet you, Michael."

"It's very nice to meet you too, Marta."

I stood up and looked around. A clothesline had been hung up on one side of the roof and someone had their wash hanging off of it. On the street below, some boys were playing stickball. Michael picked up his crutches and leaned up on them and came up beside me. He looked down at the street and watched the boys playing.

"They're the ones that locked me up here. The boy with the blue shirt on is Petey Sherwood. The kid holding the bat is Charlie Schroeder and the kid pitching to him is Harry Benson. A few years ago, we used to be friends, but since I got sick, they don't come around anymore. I guess I make them uncomfortable. They must've seen me up here looking down at the street. I saw them disappear into the building and then I heard the bolt click on the door. I could hear them laughing as they ran back down the stairs, and that's when I started pounding on the door. I didn't want my mom coming home and finding me up here alone with just my crutches."

I moved away from the wall. I didn't want them looking up and seeing us both up here and locking the door again. As far as they knew, Michael was still up here by himself.

"When do you go to school? If you come up here after your mom leaves, when do you do your schoolwork?"

I moved back over to the chairs so that Michael could sit down again and rest his legs. I had the feeling that he wouldn't sit down unless I did too. He surprised me by leaping up onto the wall to sit with his back to the street.

"Don't worry, I won't fall off. I sit up here a lot. I don't go to school anymore. My mom picks up my lessons from the school and teaches me here at home. I had missed a lot of school when I was sick and now she thinks it would be too hard for me to get around with my legs the way they are."

"What about your dad, what does he think?"

Michael jumped down off the wall and turned to face the bridge.

"He doesn't think anything anymore. He was killed in action during the war."

I stood up and moved over to the wall beside him, watching a bird that was hopping along the edge.

"I'm sorry to hear that. Was he in Europe when it happened?"

"No, he was on a ship in the Pacific. He was killed when a Japanese fighter plane crashed into his ship. I think that's why my mom worries about me so much. She doesn't want to lose me too. I think it was tougher on her than it was on me when I got sick."

My hand went to the locket that I wore around my neck and I thought about my own father that I had lost in the war. I barely remembered him.

"I lost my father on a ship, too, because of the war. It was very hard on my mom, so I can imagine what your mom's going through. At least we have Harry now."

Thinking about my mom, I remembered that I was supposed to help her with supper, and I hadn't even visited my grandma yet. If I hurried, I could stop in quick and say hello and then run home.

"Michael, I have to leave now. I promised my mom that I'd help her with supper and I still have to stop in at my Grandma's."

Michael picked up his crutches and started toward the door with me.

"I should be heading back downstairs too. My mom should be coming home pretty soon. She wouldn't leave me at all if it wasn't for the extra money she makes which helps pay for the doctor."

I held the door open for Michael and followed him back into the building.

"Let me help you down this time so that it won't take as long…I know you can do it on your own, but this way you'll get down faster."

I took his crutches for him and put his arm around my shoulders.

"Just put your weight on me and we'll start down."

Michael did as I suggested and we made it back down to the second floor in just a couple of minutes. I was just handing him back his crutches when a voice rose from behind me.

"What is going on here? Michael, were you just coming down from the roof? Did you just climb down those steps with your crutches? Who is this girl with you?"

I turned around to meet who I gathered was Michael's mother. She had the same auburn hair and green eyes. She did not look very happy at the moment.

"Marta, this is my mom. Mom, this is Marta, my new friend. She was helping me down the stairs, even though I can do it on my own with or without my crutches. It's okay Mom. I'm really careful. I won't fall."

I reached out to shake his mom's hand but she ignored the gesture. "It's nice to meet you, Mrs…" I realized that I had forgotten to ask Michael what his last name was. "I'm sorry, but I forgot to ask Michael his last name. I'm Marta Jamison. My Uncle Joey lives just down the hall from you and my grandparents live downstairs."

She had been pushing a wheelchair when she came up behind us. She moved it toward Michael and then grabbed his crutches.

"Michael, sit down in your chair. Marta, I don't know what gave you the idea that you know better than I do and can take my son up to the roof as you please. I can tell from your accent that you come from Germany, and I know this war we just fought started because your people thought they were better than the rest of the world."

I was stunned at his mother's words. I didn't know how to respond. Michael tried to explain to his mother.

"Mom, you don't understand…it wasn't Marta's idea…"

"Michael, be quiet. I've had a long day, and I'm too tired to argue."

The crutches were awkward for her to hold as she tried to push Michael toward their apartment.

"May I help you with those, Mrs…?" I still didn't know what to call her.

She let go of the chair so that Michael could wheel himself and adjusted the crutches in her hand.

"You can help by staying away from my son, and the name is Mrs. Rosenbaum."

CHAPTER EIGHT

The encounter with Michael's mother upset me so much, that I forgot to stop at my grandma's and just went home. As I walked into our apartment, my mother called to me from the kitchen.

"Is that you Marta? Where have you been? Harry's mother just called to ask how your day went at school, and I told her that you were supposed to be there visiting her. She said that you never showed up. I better call her back and tell her that you're okay, and then you can do some explaining, young lady."

After my mother hung up the phone, she pulled me into the kitchen with her. She had a colander filled with potatoes sitting in the sink. She opened the drawer and took out two paring knives and handed one to me.

"Here take this and start peeling. Now, what happened to you this afternoon? I can tell that something is upsetting you."

I took the knife and picked up a potato and started peeling it. I told my mom about meeting Michael and how nice it was up on the roof and that I meant to visit Harry's mom but I lost track of the time. I told her about Michael's mother and what she said to me.

"I really like Michael. He seems lonely and misses having friends. I know how he feels and it was nice for both of us to have someone our own age to talk to. But I don't think his mom will let me see him. Do you think Uncle Joey could talk to her since he knows her and Michael?"

We had finished peeling the potatoes and had placed them in a large pot. Mom filled the pot with water enough to cover the potatoes and set it on the stove to boil. She then dried her hands on a dishtowel and handed it to me.

"Dry your hands, Marta, and then come sit at the table with me. I made a pot of tea up just before you came in. Let's each have a cup and think this over."

We sat down at the table and I took the cup that Mom offered me. My mind drifted back to the roof and Michael as I poured cream and sugar into my tea and stirred it with a spoon. Mom did the same and stared into her cup as she stirred her tea.

"I'm sure Michael's mother didn't mean to be hurtful to you, Marta. From what you've been saying, it doesn't sound like she has it very easy right now. Her son loses the use of his legs from a sickness that could've killed him. Her husband is killed in a war that took your father too. At least we have someone to help us. She is doing it alone, trying to be both mother and father."

I took a sip of the hot tea. It felt nice and warm going down. I had felt chilled when I left Michael, partly from the breezy air on the roof and partly from the things his mother had said.

"I know that people are angry for the losses that they have suffered. We suffered too. But will they ever forgive, Mom?"

Mom put her teacup down and put her arms around my shoulders. She put her head next to mine.

"They have to heal first. Don't give up on Michael or his mother. We'll leave Uncle Joey out of this for now. I don't want to risk Michael losing him as a friend. Knowing your Uncle, he'll probably use his natural charm to soften Mrs. Rosenbaum anyway."

Harry came home a little while later and asked me how school was. I showed him my books and after supper he helped me with my homework. I told him about what happened with Michael and his mother.

"Would you like me to go over there and talk to Mrs. Rosenbaum?"

"No, that's okay Dad. Mom and I decided that it would be better not to push her too much where Michael is concerned. Mom feels that she'll come around. You know that I am such a likeable girl."

I batted my eyelashes and crossed my eyes as I said this to Harry. I was feeling much better and I hoped that Michael was okay too. Harry laughed at my antics and pulled lightly on one of my braids.

"Yes you are very likeable, Marta. You take after your very loveable mother."

The days passed, and soon the weekend arrived. It was nice to sleep in an extra hour on Saturday morning. A noise awakened me from my slumber and I opened my eyes to find another pair of eyes staring back. It was a kitten, a calico just like my Minka in Germany. She mewed at me and I picked her up as I sat up in my bed.

"Where did you come from little one?"

Harry and mom came in then and sat on the edge of my bed. Harry reached over to pet the kitten.

"Do you like her, Marta? Mrs. Rossilini keeps a cat at her bakery to keep away the mice. She just had a litter of kittens, the cat, that is, not Mrs. Rossilini, and she asked if we'd like one. This one reminded me of the cat you had in Germany."

I nuzzled the kitten with my face and then placed her on the bed where she ran in a circle chasing her tail.

"She's adorable. I love her. Thanks so much. I think I'll call her Muffin, since she came from a bakery."

I jumped out of bed and got washed up and dressed. I held Muffin on my lap during breakfast, though Harry and Mom advised me that it wouldn't be a daily occurrence. I snuck her a bite of my eggs and a drop of my milk. I spent the day setting up her litter box and food area and playing with her.

After supper, Harry and mom decided to go to a movie. I didn't feel like going and I wanted to stay with Muffin on her first night in our home.

"Are you sure you don't mind being alone, Marta? I could get my mom or Louise to come over and keep you company."

"No, Harry, I don't mind, besides I'm not alone, Muffin will be here, too. I have some homework I can do and I can read that new Archie comic book that you bought me today. I'll be fine. Which movie are you going to?"

Mom came into the room adjusting her hat and pulling on her gloves.

"Harry wants to see "Duel in the Sun," but I would rather see "The Farmer's Daughter.""

I looked over at Harry's besotted face, which he wore every time my mom walked into the room.

"I hope Harry enjoys "The Farmer's Daughter"."

Muffin curled up next to me on my bed while I lay down on my side and read my comic book. After awhile I felt restless and started thinking about Michael. I looked over at the kitten sleeping peacefully by my pillow and decided to take a walk. I thought about going up the stairs to our roof to look at the stars, but decided that there was another rooftop out there that I would enjoy a lot more.

Grabbing a sweater to wear, I made sure I had my key in the right pocket of my dungarees and locked the door as I left. I walked the few blocks over to my grandparents' home. I passed their apartment and climbed the stairs to the second floor. I didn't hear any noise coming from Uncle Joey's apartment and wondered if he was home. I looked up the stairs leading to the roof and placed my foot on the first step, and then paused for a minute to decide whether to continue or not. My feet seemed to decide before my brain did because before I knew it I was opening the door and walking outside on the rooftop.

Uncle Joey stood by a wall with Michael, who was in his wheelchair. They were looking up at the bridge. They didn't hear me come out at first and continued to talk to each other.

"The bridge sure looks neat at night, doesn't it Joey? My dad and I used to come out here all the time to look at it. Sometimes on a Sunday afternoon, we'd walk across the bridge and look out at the boats. I sure miss that. I hope I can walk across it again someday."

Joey put his arm around Michael and placed his hand on his shoulder.

"You will kid, but just remember to always cross back again to this side of the bridge. There ain't no place like home, and Brooklyn is home and where the heart is."

"You sound like a poet, Uncle Joey. You should write an 'Ode to Brooklyn'."

Joey was startled as I came up behind him and Michael. He relaxed when he recognized me. He turned Michael's chair around to face me.

"Geez, Marta, I didn't hear you come out here. I thought you were Mrs. Rosenbaum. She doesn't like Michael sitting so close to the edge. And yeah, you're right. I've *owed* my whole life to Brooklyn."

Michael and I both looked at each other and tried to keep a straight face. We didn't know if Uncle Joey was making a pun, or really misunderstood when I said 'ode'.

"Hello Michael, how have you been doing?"

"I'm doing okay, Marta. I'm sorry about Mother the other day. I did explain to her that I was already up here when you found me, but that didn't seem to make her mood any better."

Uncle Joey sat on the wall, listening to Michael and me talk. He already knew about the encounter I had with Michael's mother from Grandma, who found out from Mom.

After a few minutes, he stood up and started heading toward the door.

"You kids chat for awhile. I'm just going to run downstairs and check on Helen. The doctor says it could be any day now, and I don't like leaving her alone too long. I'll be right back."

After Harry left, Michael followed me over to the lawn chairs, and I sat down and tugged my sweater closer around me.

"It's getting a bit chilly up here, but it's so beautiful. You were right about the stars, Michael. I really do feel like I could reach up and pluck one out of the sky. And the bridge, I've never seen it lit up like that before."

Michael looked up at the sky and smiled.

"It helps keep me sane through my days of confinement. If I couldn't come up here once and awhile, I'd probably go bonkers."

"Your mother probably thinks you already are bonkers when she found out that you come up here on crutches by yourself. Is she still upset with me, Michael? I was afraid of running into her tonight, in case she'd keep me from seeing you."

Michael looked down at his legs for a few minutes, seeming to be deep in thought. He then looked up at me and reached for my hand.

"Don't worry about my mother, Marta. I don't want you to stop coming around to see me. You're the first friend I've had in a long time, besides Joey of course, but he's a grown-up. It's nice to have someone my own age to talk to. I don't think my mom really dislikes you. I just think that she's afraid for me. She saw how all my other friends stopped coming around after I got sick and she doesn't want me to be hurt again. Please say that you'll keep coming over."

Marta got up from her chair and walked over to look out at the night view. She could hear Michael wheeling himself up behind her. She turned around and leaned against the wall and smiled.

"I'll keep coming back, Michael. You're the first friend I've made in a long time, too. I hate having to sneak behind your mom's back, but, hopefully, we won't have to for long. I'll come back next week after school."

Uncle Joey came back as I was getting ready to leave.

"Hey, Mikey, I just heard some of the game on the radio downstairs. Looks like the Cardinals and Boston for the '46 World Series. Who would've thought the Red Sox would make it this far? Hey, Marty, you already leaving?"

"Mom and Dad went to the movies tonight and should be home pretty soon. I don't want them to worry if I'm not there when they get home."

She walked over to the door and opened it. Before leaving, she turned to Michael and waved.

"So long, Michael, or as we say in Germany...*tschus* for now. Goodnight Uncle Joey."

Marta then left and closed the door behind her. She listened for a minute at the door before descending the steps. She smiled as she heard Michael and Uncle Joey talking.

"*Choos*? What the heck does that mean Michael?"

"I think it means I'll be seeing her again."

CHAPTER NINE

I ran home and let myself into our apartment. Muffin was still curled up by my pillow. I undressed and put on my nightgown and brushed my teeth. I undid my braids and while I was brushing my hair, I could hear Mom and Dad coming in.

"Marta, we're home. I brought you some popcorn from the movies."

I put down my brush and went out into the living room. Harry handed me the popcorn and I put some in my mouth.

"This is good. It's really buttery. Thanks. What movie did you decide to see?"

Mom took off her hat and gloves and placed them by her purse on the side table.

"We saw "The Farmer's Daughter, who was played by the actress Loretta Young. She was very good. It was a nice movie. Make sure you brush your teeth after eating that popcorn, Marta."

I finished the last piece of corn and licked the butter off my fingers.

"I already did, Mom. Just before you came in."

Mom came over and inspected my fingers that still had remnants of popcorn and butter on them.

"Then you'll have to brush them again. Wash your fingers too while you're at it…with soap, not your tongue."

The next morning, we arose and went to Church as usual. During the service, the minister made an announcement about a neighborhood block party that some members of the church were putting together to raise money for the homeless. They were asking for donations of food and drinks and they were going to have games for kids and a bake sale and a raffle for prizes that some of the local businesses were donating. It sounded like it was going to be a lot of fun. I hoped that Michael's mother would let him attend.

We went to Harry's parents, and this week Uncle Joey and Aunt Helen joined us. Uncle Joey looked very nervous. He kept staring at Aunt Helen and following her around the room.

"Oh do sit down, Joey. You're driving me crazy. I can still call for you from across the room if I need you. Stop being so nervous."

"Yeah, that's easy for you to say, Helen. You're not about to become a father."

"You're right, Joey. What was I thinking? All that pacing back and forth you'll be doing at the hospital, tiring yourself out. All I'll be doing is giving birth."

After dinner, Uncle Joey and Aunt Helen went back upstairs to their apartment. Before they left, I asked Uncle Joey if he'd seen Michael around today.

"They always go to Mrs. Rosenbaum's sister on Sundays. His Uncle Paulie picks them up and brings them back in the evening. Come on Helen, let's get you upstairs so you can rest."

After they left, I went into the kitchen to help with the dishes. Aunt Louise washed while I dried. We talked about school, both hers and mine.

"So Marta, are ya meeting a lot of kids in your class?"

I grabbed the plate she was handing me and started drying it.

"It's only been a week so far, but I'm getting to know the other kids. They kind of kept to themselves in the beginning. I guess most of these kids have known each other since kindergarten. But, some of them have started to talk to me, and one girl named Jenny invited me to sit next to her at lunch. She wears glasses and has braces on her teeth, and sometimes the other kids tease her. She was very nice to me, and now I have someone to eat lunch with."

Aunt Louise placed the roasting pan in the sink to soak after handing me the last of the glasses to dry.

"I remember well what kids can be like in grammar school. They can be so cruel with their teasing. At least most of them outgrow it by the time they get to college; though I've met some boys at college who can be pretty immature."

We finished up the dishes and made coffee to have with the chocolate cake my mom made. Aunt Louise told me stories about some of the people she knew at college. She was very good at describing people, and I told her that I'd love to read some of the articles she'd written for her college newspaper.

"When we finish with dessert, we can go into my room and I'll let you read my scrapbook. I keep clippings of all my articles together in a book, so I'll have it handy when I start interviewing for a job after I graduate next year."

Later on, when we returned home, I couldn't find Muffin anywhere. Harry and Mom helped me look for her. We looked everywhere that we could think of. I looked under my bed and in my closet, and we searched under all the furniture in the living room and in the cupboards in the kitchen. I was very upset, but Mom told me that it was getting late and to get ready for bed.

"I'm sure she'll turn up eventually, especially when she gets hungry."

I went to my room to undress. As I opened my dresser drawer to pull out a clean nightgown, I found Muffin curled up inside. She opened up one eye, mewed, and then went back to sleep. I lifted her out and put her next to my pillow on my bed.

Monday morning it was raining as Harry and I walked together to school. He would leave me at my corner by my school and continue on to work. We shared an umbrella, and then I told Harry to take it with him. The hooded rain jacket I wore kept me dry.

Because of the rain, the schoolyard was empty. Everyone would be in the gymnasium until the bell rang for classes to begin. I went through the side doors and could hear the noise of hundreds of kids echoing through the halls. I saw Jenny standing by the gymnasium door and I went over to talk to her. Her face lit up and she smiled when I approached her.

"Pretty wet out there today. How are you, Jenny?"

"Oh, I'm okay. I hate it when it rains and we have to come inside. It gets so crowded with everyone packed into the gym. Especially when those boys over there play tag and run all over and into everybody. That's why I stand over here, it's safer."

I looked over at the boys she was pointing at. I recognized Petey, Charlie and Harry, Michael's ex-buddies. From the way they were running into kids and laughing when they knocked them down, I didn't think Michael was missing much.

"Come on, Jenny. We can go in and play something if you'd like. I see some balls and jump-ropes over on the benches."

Jenny looked horrified at the suggestion. She backed away as I tried to nudge her into the gym.

"No, that's okay, Marta. I'd rather just wait here until the bell rings. I'm sort of clumsy when it comes to playing games. They make fun enough of my glasses and the braces on my teeth. I wouldn't want to give them any more ammunition."

I felt bad for Jenny. Aunt Louise was right. Sometimes kids can be so cruel to other kids.

"I like your glasses, Jenny. The braces on your teeth don't look so bad. I think you're very pretty."

Jenny shook her head and looked down at the floor.

"You don't have to say that, Marta. I know I'm not pretty. You're the one that's pretty, with your long blonde braids and blue eyes. You can't even see the color of my eyes through these glasses and my mouth is a metallic nightmare."

I took Jenny's hand and made her follow me into the girl's room down the hall.

"Come over here, Jenny and look in the mirror. Tell me what you see."

She didn't want to and started to leave. "I already told you what I see. A four-eyed metal mouth. Now leave me alone."

I gently pushed her over to the mirror that hung over the washbasin. She wouldn't raise her eyes up from the sink.

"Look again. Can I tell you what I see? I see a girl who has lovely brown eyes that looked upon a girl that was a stranger to a new country and befriended her. I see someone with a beautiful smile that shines not from the metal on your teeth, but from the kindness in your heart. You are a very pretty girl, Jenny, inside and out and don't let anyone else ever tell you different."

At that moment the bell rang for class. Jenny glanced up at the mirror and stared for a moment. She nodded her head at me, and then smiled as she followed me out into the hall. As we made our way to class, Petey Sherwood shoved into her as he tried to pass by us.

"Get out of the way four-eyes!"

I held my breath as I waited for Jenny's reaction to what that creep, Petey, said to her. She stuck her foot out and tripped him.

"Tsk, Tsk...you should watch where you're going, Petey. I think that you're the one that needs four eyes."

The morning dragged by slowly. When it was finally time for lunch, I was more than ready for it. It had stopped raining, so Jenny and I walked around the schoolyard after we finished eating. Mary was out there with her usual circle of friends. She ignored Jenny and me as we walked by. Ever since that first day of school, she stayed away from me. The few times on Sunday afternoons that we are forced to be together at Harry's parents are spent with us being coolly polite with each other. Especially, since Harry sits between us.

That afternoon, I ran home and dropped my schoolbag off and asked my mom if I could go visit Michael.

"Has his mother said it's okay for you to see him?"

"Well, I haven't really seen her since that day, but I promised Michael that I'd still come by. He gets really lonely there by himself. If Mrs. Rosenbaum tells me to go back home, I will. I promise."

Marta didn't bother telling her mom that Mrs. Rosenbaum wouldn't be there and so she wouldn't have to worry about seeing her.

"Okay, but just for an hour. Then you need to come home and start your homework. You still have that report to do for social studies."

I climbed the stairs up to the roof and opened the door. I ran out and called for Michael. He wasn't there. I walked all around. There was no trace of him. I didn't know what to do. Should I knock on his door and see if he's okay? What if his mother answered? I guess the most she could do to me is slam the door in my face.

I went back down the stairs and walked down the hall to Michael's apartment. I hesitated for a moment and then I raised my hand to the door and knocked. I could hear movement inside.

"Who is it?"

I was relieved that it was Michael's voice. He sounded okay.

"It's Marta. Are you alright?"

"Come on in, Marta."

I opened the door and walked inside. Michael was sitting in his wheelchair by the window reading a comic book. I looked around for his mother.

"She's not home. She's at work right now."

I moved over to where he was sitting and sat down on the window seat.

"How come you weren't upstairs today?"

"It rained today, and the puddles make it slippery up there for me on my crutches, so I decided to just stay in here and read."

I picked up the comic book he was reading. It was a Superman comic.

"If you'd like, I could help you up there."

I heard a patter on the window and we both looked out to see the rain starting again.

"On second thought, maybe it would be better to stay inside today. Will your mother be home soon?"

"Not for another two hours. Do you want to play a game?"

I put his comic book back down and got up from the window seat.

"Sure, what do you want to play?"

He turned his chair toward the kitchen and motioned me to follow him.

"Grab that game off the shelf and we'll play on the kitchen table. Have you ever played Monopoly?"

I picked up the game that he pointed to and followed him into the kitchen. I placed it on the table and sat down in one of the chairs while Michael wheeled his chair in across from me.

"No, I've never played this game. You will have to tell me what to do."

A gleam appeared in Michael's eyes as he lifted the lid off the box and started taking out the game pieces.

"Sure, no problem. I get to be the banker and I'll explain as we go along. Here is your Monopoly money...now let's see...you really don't want to buy Park Place or Boardwalk..."

We had a good time playing the game. Michael was beating me, as I payed him most of my money each time I landed on Park Place. I didn't care. We talked about our favorite comic books. I like the Archie comics, but Michael prefers the super hero ones.

"There's this comic book character called *the Claw*. He's this monster with these amazing powers who's out to dominate the universe. But don't worry. He gets defeated."

I threw the dice and counted the spaces. Once again, I landed on Park Place.

"The Claw sort of reminds me of someone else who was defeated."

Michael looked at me puzzled for a second and then enlightenment struck him. We just finished a war that was started by a monster.

When the game was over, I helped Michael put the pieces away and placed it back on the shelf.

"I better get going. Your mom should be home in a little while and I have a report to do. I'll stop by again tomorrow if that's okay."

Michael saw me to the door and let me out.

"That'll be great. Hopefully, it won't rain tomorrow. If it does we can always play another game. How are you at chess?"

"Probably just as good as I was at Monopoly. I guess I better pray for sunshine then. See you tomorrow, Michael."

"Choos, Marta!"

I smiled at him for remembering the word I used the other night when I said goodnight to him on the roof.

"Tschuss, Michael!"

CHAPTER TEN

The weekend was approaching, and everyone in the neighborhood was getting ready for the block party. The forecast said it was going to be sunny on Saturday. The block party was set to start in the afternoon and go on late into the night.

Mom made four cakes to donate to the bake sale and Mrs. Jacobs made six-dozen oatmeal and raisin cookies. I asked Michael if his mom was letting him go to the party. He said that she had to work in the afternoon, but that she'd take him for a little while in the evening.

Saturday morning, I got up early and helped Mom frost the cakes for the bake sale. She made two chocolate, an angel food, and a bundt cake. When afternoon finally arrived, I helped Mom and Harry carry them downstairs. Dressed in my usual Saturday dungarees and a pink sweater that my grandma had bought for me, I was ready to play and have a good time.

The street had been blocked off from traffic at both ends, and all the cars that were normally parked in front of the apartments were moved to another street. The party wasn't just limited to the residents of our street. Everybody from the congregation was invited, and from the way the street was filling up, it looked like everybody came. Even though Michael and his mother were Jewish and didn't belong to our church, it didn't matter. They still belonged to our neighborhood.

They had games set up along the street for the kids to play. There was a ring toss. Mr. Nichols donated Coca Cola from his grocery store and if the ring landed on a bottle, you'd win the pop. I watched some of the other kids play first and then I decided to try. Harry had given me some nickels to use for playing some of the games. I made it on my second try and won the soda.

Farther down the street was a balloon game. The balloons had been blown up with a piece of paper inside that named a prize. If you hit the balloon with a dart and popped it, you won the prize on the piece of paper. I saw Jenny on line to play this game. I went over and waited behind her. She threw a dart at one of the balloons, while her parents watched. The balloon popped and her parents clapped while Jenny got her prize. She won a pack of chewing gum. She laughed when she saw me and handed the gum to me.

"I can just imagine trying to chew this gum with my braces. They'd probably have to pry my mouth open afterwards."

I took the gum and told her to wait while I tried to pop a balloon.

"Since you gave me your prize, if I win you can have whatever my prize is. Hopefully, it won't be more gum."

I took the two darts that they gave you to throw. The first one didn't pop the balloon, but the second one did. My prize was a small pink hand mirror. I handed it to Jenny.

"Here, take this to remind yourself every time you look in it of how pretty you really are."

She took the mirror and held it up to her face. Then she put it in her pocket and gave me a hug. I waved goodbye to her as she followed her parents over to the refreshment stand.

There were more games, but I didn't feel like playing anymore. I thought of Michael, and I decided to go and see him. I found Mom and Harry sitting at one of the tables that had been set up for people to sit and listen to the music and enjoy a snack. The music consisted of a drummer and a sax player, and a man on a piano that had been brought over on the back of a truck. I told them where I was going and they nodded and said to check back with them in a little while.

"Don't stay away too long, Marta. Soon as it gets dark and the lights come on, there's going to be dancing. I've already been promised a dance or two with your mom. I was hoping to get to dance one with you too."

"I'm not much of a dancer, Dad. But if you're willing to risk it, so am I."

It took awhile to get through the street with all the people. Once I rounded the corner to Michael's street, I was able to run the rest of the way. I ran up the steps of his front stoop and hurried inside. The building was quiet. Everybody was at the party. As I climbed the stairs to the second floor, Uncle Joey rushed past me down the steps pulling Aunt Helen along behind him.

"Are you going to the party, Uncle Joey?"

"Looks like we're going to have a party of our own tonight at the hospital, Marty. The baby's coming."

"Oh, Aunt Helen, how exciting. Uncle Joey, do you want me to go get Harry and your parents?"

"Nah, Marty. That's okay. Let them have some fun. There's not much they can do at the hospital anyway. You can let them know when you see them that we're at the hospital and I'll call as soon as the baby's born."

Carrying a little suitcase in one hand, Uncle Joey opened the front door with the other and held it for his wife.

"Oh geez, where are the car keys?"

"They're in your hand, Joey. Now get me to the hospital before I have this baby on the front stoop."

I watched them leave, excited about a new baby in the family. I climbed the rest of the steps to the second floor. I wondered if Michael would be in his apartment or on the roof. I decided on the latter and went up the second set of steps and opened the door. Michael was standing there, leaning on his crutches by the wall, looking out at the bridge. He turned around when he heard me close the door.

"Hi, Marta. I thought that you'd be at the party."

I held up the coke and the pack of chewing gum.

"I was and I won this pop and my friend Jenny gave me this pack of gum that she won. She can't chew gum with her braces. I thought I'd come up here and share them with you. We're going to need a bottle opener though."

Michael took the soda bottle from me and leaned the top of it against the edge of the wall. He popped the top off and handed it back to me.

"My dad taught me that when we used to drink pop up here at night."

I handed the bottle back to him.

"Well, since you opened it, you have the honor of the first sip."

He took the bottle back and held it up to his mouth and took a gulp. Then he handed it back to me. We passed it back and forth until it was all gone. I unwrapped the gum then, and handed him a piece.

"Thanks. Tell me about the party. What kind of stuff do they have?"

"All kinds of stuff, but first I have to tell you that I ran into Uncle Joey and Aunt Helen on the way up here. They were on their way to the hospital because the baby is coming."

"That's great! I don't think Joey could've lasted much longer."

We sat and talked for a while. I told Michael all about the games and the music and all the people that filled the street.

"I wish that I could take you there with me Michael. When is your mom going to be back? She did say she'd take you tonight, didn't she?"

"That's none of your business, young lady. I thought I told you to stay away from Michael."

Michael and I turned around to see his mother standing by the door looking at us. We both must've looked surprised. We hadn't heard her come up the steps.

"Hello, Mrs. Rosenbaum. It's a very nice day today, isn't it? I was just telling Michael about the party and how it will be so much fun when you bring him."

Mrs. Rosenbaum looked at Michael sitting on one of the lawn chairs, his crutches lying on the floor next to him.

"You better leave, Marta. Michael, you disobeyed me. Forget about any party."

Michael's face fell as his mother came over and picked up his crutches. She handed them to him as he stood up and then helped him to the door. I followed behind as she helped Michael down the steps.

"Michael won't be coming tonight. You'd better leave now."

I watched them walk down the hall and go into their apartment. I felt so disappointed for Michael and for myself. I slowly made my way down to the first floor and out the door. I sat down on the front stoop, not feeling like going back to the party. I sat there for a while, until I heard someone coming down the stairs from the second floor. I knew it had to be Mrs. Rosenbaum, since no one else but Michael was home. I got up and quickly hid behind a car that was parked on the street in front of the building.

I watched Michael's mother come down the steps and go down the street. I wondered where she was going since the beauty parlor where she worked would be closed now. I guessed that she was probably going to the store for something. If that was the case, she'd be back soon. Against my better judgment, I ran back up to see Michael.

When I got to his apartment door, I knocked and waited to be let in. No one answered and I couldn't hear any movement inside. I was puzzled about what to do next. He couldn't be on the roof again. Or could he? I made my way up the stairs again. When I came outside, there was no one there. He must be in his apartment. I would've seen him if he left the building. I guess he must be in his room and wants to be left alone. I couldn't blame him right now. I walked over to the edge and looked down at the street. Petey, Charlie and Harry were sitting on the stoop of the building next door. Petey was showing them something and they were all laughing.

Oh well, at least someone was having a good time.

I went back downstairs and headed back to our street. I didn't feel like being at the party anymore. I was going to go find Mom and Harry and tell them that I wanted to go home. I could always work on my report. It was due Monday, and I still hadn't finished it yet.

As I got to the corner, I looked back at Michael's building before turning onto my own street. The boys weren't sitting on the steps anymore. I didn't see them on the street anywhere either. Well, they couldn't hurt Michael. He wasn't on the roof for them to lock him up there. I turned the corner and walked over to where Mom and Harry were. They were dancing a slow dance together. I watched them for a few minutes and then went up to our building. I walked inside and decided to go up to the roof.

I climbed the steps and opened the door that led out to the roof of our building. I walked over to the edge and looked down at the people on the street below. Evening was approaching, and the streetlights were starting to come on. Everything looks so different from up here. I could see Harry and Mom dancing. The glow of the streetlights reflecting on their blonde hair made it look as if two angels were dancing. Other people stopped to watch them dance. They were a beautiful site to behold.

I looked across the other rooftops until I spotted Michael's building. I noticed a flicker of light coming off the roof. Michael must have been up there and brought a light with him.

I decided to go and see him one more time tonight. His mother mustn't be back yet, r he wouldn't be up there. I knew that he must be feeling pretty lonely and depressed right now and I needed to try and cheer him up.

I went back down to the street and worked my way once again through the crowd of people. Once I got to the corner, I ran again to Michael's. I looked down the street to see if Mrs. Rosenbaum was coming. Seeing no one in sight, I continued on. Once I got inside, I slowed down as I climbed the steps to the second floor.

Nearing the steps that led to the roof, I started smelling something strange in the air.

As I climbed the steps, the roof door swung open. Petey and his two friends were coming from the roof. I realized what the strange smell was; smoke. They ran past me down the steps. Charlie was yelling at Petey.

"I told you we shouldn't have fired that second rocket. Let's get out of here!"

I shouted after them, but they kept on going down the stairs to the first floor. "What's going on? Where's Michael?"

I could hear the front door shut as they ran out of the building. That familiar tightness crept inside me, but this time it wasn't fear for myself, but for someone else. Michael!

I rushed up the steps and opened the door and stepped out onto the roof. There was smoke everywhere. I looked all around yelling for Michael. When I came to the other side of the roof where the clothesline hung, I saw fire. Someone's wash that had been hanging there was burning. A breeze coming across the roof was spreading it fast. There was no sign of Michael.

The smoke was getting thicker as I hurried back toward the door. I flew down the steps and ran down the hall to Michael's apartment. I didn't hesitate this time before knocking. I raised my hand and started pounding on the door. I tried the knob and the door was unlocked. I opened it and went inside.

"Michael, are you in here?"

I heard a noise coming from the direction of the bedrooms. Michael opened his bedroom door. He was in his wheelchair, holding a comic book on his lap.

"What's wrong Marta?"

"Michael, the roof is on fire. It looks like Petey and his friends were shooting off some type of fireworks. We've got to get out of here. Where's your mom?"

Michael threw down his comic book and wheeled himself out to the living room.

"Hand me the crutches by the couch. My mom had to go back to the shop and clean the floors. She was going to do it tomorrow, but since she was mad at me, she thought she'd go back tonight and finish. Shouldn't we call the fire department?"

I handed him his crutches and helped him out of the chair.

"Let's get out of here first and then we'll find a phone."

Using his crutches, Michael followed me out of his apartment. The hall was already filled with smoke as we made our way toward the stairs leading down to the first floor. When we got to the staircase, I took Michael's crutches and threw them down ahead of us. I then told him to grab the railing with his left hand and lean on me and I'd help him down the steps. We took each step together and by the time we got to the bottom, we could already hear sirens coming down the street. Someone else must've seen the smoke and called the fire department.

As I leaned down to pick up his crutches, the front door opened and two firemen rushed in. One of them took Michael and helped him out. The other ran up the stairs toward the fire. When I got outside, I could see Mrs. Rosenbaum down the block, running toward us. Harry and Mom were rushing toward me from across the street, Harry's parents following behind.

"Marta, are you okay? What happened?"

"It's okay, Mom. Some boys started a fire on the roof, but Michael and I got out okay. It was a good thing that no one else was in the building."

Grandma looked up at the burning building and started to shake.

"Oh no, Joey and Helen are still up there. They didn't come to the street party."

Harry was about to push his way through the crowd that was gathering to run inside. I grabbed his arm and tugged him back.

"It's okay, dad. Uncle Joey and Aunt Helen left for the hospital a while ago. Helen was having the baby. I passed them on the stairs when I came here earlier. They were gone way before the fire even started."

When Grandma heard this, she calmed down. She then smiled with relief and hugged me.

"Thank goodness. Well, we should all head to the hospital and see if that baby's been born yet. Knowing Joey, he's probably driving the nurses crazy by now."

Grandpa was going to drive us in his car. I asked them to wait for me and that I'd be right back. I left them standing by the car, watching the firemen go back and forth from the building. I had to see how Michael was doing. I pushed my way through the crowd and found them sitting on the back of an ambulance, watching the firemen as they hosed down the roof. I walked over to where they were sitting, hoping that Mrs. Rosenbaum wasn't still angry.

"Michael, are you okay? Mrs. Rosenbaum, I'm so sorry."

Michael was watching a fireman attaching another hose to the hydrant. He looked up and smiled when he saw me.

"I'm okay, Marta. They just brought me back here to make sure I didn't hurt my legs coming down the stairs. They want me to stay here until they can get my wheelchair down to me."

I looked over at Mrs. Rosenbaum and then back at Michael. He rolled his eyes at me as his mom kept hugging him to her.

"I'm alright, Mom. You don't have to keep squeezing me so tight."

Mrs. Rosenbaum let go of Michael and wiped tears from her face.

"I know dear, but when I saw the fire trucks turning down our street, I thought my heart would stop. When I saw you and Marta coming out of the very building that was on fire, I think it did stop."

"Thanks to Marta, I made it out okay. She came and got me out before the smoke got too thick."

Mrs. Rosenbaum looked at me and it was the first time that I'd ever seen her smile. She stood up and stepped down from the back of the ambulance truck, and put her arms around me and hugged me. I looked over her shoulder at Michael who broke out into a big grin. I wasn't sure if that was because his mother finally let go of him or that it looked like she was finally accepting me. I didn't care. I hugged her back.

"Thank you dear for helping Michael. I'm sorry about the way I've been acting but I just worry about Michael so much. It's been hard since his father died. You can come and see him anytime you want. You can come and see both of us."

I pulled away from her gently and smiled back at her.

"That would be great, Mrs. Rosenbaum. What are you both going to do if you can't get back into your apartment tonight? We're all going to the hospital now.

Uncle Joey and Aunt Helen left for the hospital before the fire broke out and we want to wait there with him until the baby is born. That's if it hasn't happened already."

"That's wonderful, dear. You must say hi to your Uncle Joey for us when you see him. We'll be okay. Mrs. Janovich down the block let me use her phone. I called my sister in New Jersey and her husband Paul is coming to pick us up. We'll be staying there for the night."

One of the firemen came down the front steps carrying a wheelchair. Mrs. Rosenbaum moved over to take it from him and set it down on the sidewalk while the fireman helped Michael off the ambulance and into his chair.

"I guess while we're waiting, we can go to the street party for awhile. I still hear music playing over there and I bet there's still lots of Cotton Candy and Popcorn left at the stands."

Michael looked at me and reached out his arm. I leaned over and hugged him.

"I wish you could come with us, Marta. We could share another coke."

"I know Michael, but I think this is time you need to spend with just your mom. I have to be going anyway. They're waiting for me by the car. I'll let you know if it's a boy or a girl."

I waved goodbye to both of them and made my way back to Grandpa's car. I saw Harry talking to a fireman and when he saw me he nodded to the man and then walked toward me.

"Looks like the fire was contained on the roof. There's a lot of smoke that still has to be cleared out but everybody should be able to get back inside by tomorrow. They want to know if you saw who it was who set off the fireworks."

I nodded and went with Harry to talk to the Fire Chief. I told him what I saw when I came into the building. They were going to talk to the boys' parents that night and let them know what happened.

We walked back to the car and Harry opened the door for me so that I could climb in back with Aunt Louise and Grandma. Mom sat in the front between Harry and Grandpa.

We drove to the hospital and parked next to Uncle Joey's car in the parking lot. We found him pacing in the waiting room. When he saw us he stopped and sat down in one of the chairs.

"It's been three hours and I still haven't heard anything. What's taking so long?"

Mom and Grandma looked at each other and smiled.

"These things take time, Joey, especially when it's your first child. Why, I was in labor with you for nine hours, and you've never given me a moment's peace since."

This she said as she put her arms around Joey and hugged him. We all sat down and waited with Joey. Harry went down to the cafeteria and brought back some juice for me, and coffee for the others. We told Joey about the fire.

"Well, they said that Helen will have to stay ten days in the hospital after the baby is born. They usually keep all new mothers for that long. That'll give me time to make sure all the baby stuff is clean and smoke free."

Another hour passed before a nurse finally came into the waiting area.

"Mr. Jamison?"

Harry and Grandpa and Joey all stood up at the same time.

The nurse looked at the three of them, a confused expression appearing on her face.

"I'm looking for the Mr. Jamison whose wife just had a baby boy."

CHAPTER ELEVEN

A month has passed since Jimmy Jamison came into the world. Aunt Helen named her son after the brother she lost. She's been a lot happier these days. Last Sunday, she let me hold the baby and asked me if I'd like to baby-sit for them sometime. Mrs. Jacobs was right about Aunt Helen. She really does have a good heart. I think having the baby helped her to get over the loss of her older brother.

I've been doing better at school. As I become more fluent in my new language, I find the schoolwork much easier to do. Jenny's braces came off last week. Now she smiles all the time. We have lunch together every day and a couple of other girls have sat down at our table and joined us.

Mrs. Rosenbaum let Michael return to school. The janitor set up some ramps outside the school to make it easier for him to use his wheelchair. I like having him in my class, and he's making new friends again. Petey, Charlie and Harry have been well behaved since the night of the fire. They even help Michael get around the school. I think what happened that night really scared them. Mary still ignores me, but I'm not giving up on her either. We are cousins already; hopefully someday we'll be friends too.

*   *   *   *

The sound of my mother laughing woke me. It's Saturday morning and Muffin is jumping on my face right now.

"Okay, okay. I'll get up and feed you."

I got out of bed and walked into the kitchen, carrying Muffin with me. Harry and Mom were dancing in the kitchen to a slow tune that was playing on the radio.

"Kind of early to be dancing, isn't it, Mom?"

Harry turned and looked at me and escorted my mother to one of the kitchen chairs.

"It's never too early for dancing with the one you love. Your mother just gave me some great news. She's going to have a baby."

I ran over to my mom and threw my arms around her.

"Mom, that's great. Looks like little Jimmy will have a playmate soon."

We sat down to a breakfast of heavenly hard rolls from Mrs. Rossilini's bakery.

Later on that afternoon, I asked Harry if he'd do me a favor.

"You just have to ask, Marta. You know I'd do anything I can for you and I'm in an especially generous mood today."

I told him what I wanted to do and he smiled at me and said, "No problem. That's a great idea."

It is now Saturday night, and I'm standing on the Brooklyn Bridge with Michael. Harry gave us a ride in Uncle Joey's car. He and Mrs. Rosenbaum are waiting for us by the car.

"Okay, Michael…you ready?"

I helped Michael out of his wheelchair and handed him his crutches. Tonight we're walking across the Brooklyn Bridge together.

"Okay Michael, let's go…one step at a time."

Second Chance

Gabriel sat behind the desk in his office. Golden light was streaming through the skylight, creating a heavenly glow. A bell rang somewhere on the desk and he reached over to press the intercom.

"Yes, Sera, what is it?"

"Milicent is here as you requested, sir."

"Good, good. Please send her in."

"Very well, sir. Would you care for some coffee?"

"Yes, Sera, thank you…and maybe some of your divine Angel food cake?"

He stood up and walked to a set of doors, which opened as he neared them. Waiting there was a woman dressed in a long white robe with gray hair rolled into a bun at the back of her head.

"Milicent, good to see you. Come, sit down. Sera is bringing us some refreshments. Here she is now."

A beautiful woman with silver blond hair, wearing a robe similar to Milicent's but blue instead of white, entered. She placed the tray she carried on the desk between Gabriel and Milicent.

"Will there be anything else, sir?"

Gabriel reached for the coffee and handed a cup to Milicent.

"No, that's fine, Sera, thank you."

Sera smiled as she looked back at them and closed the doors behind her.

Milicent took the cup that Gabriel offered but refused the cake.

"I can't help wondering why I'm here, Gabriel. You seem to be trying to soften me up." Milicent felt at ease calling him by his name. She ranked very high as Angels go. Not as high as Gabriel, but much higher than most. Angels wore different colored robes according to their position. Silver for Archangels like Gabriel, white for the teachers who guided the others. New students wore brown. They still have to earn their "wings" before they graduate to blue.

Gabriel put his empty plate down and looked over at Milicent.

"I have an assignment for one of your pupils. A young girl that's having a difficult time is running away. Providence shows us that this would put her in danger, and, though we look upon all our charges as important, this one could be disastrous. If she strays from the path planned for her it could upset an important part of the future of mankind. I believe it's one of her grandchildren that's destined to find a way to repair the hole in what they call their Ozone layer. I wish they would, I'm sick of all the drafts that drift up through it. Anyway, let's send Emmeline."

Milicent sputtered coffee as she took a sip. She put her cup down, stood up, and began to pace across the room.

"You're not serious! Emmeline? Send her on an important assignment? You know her record. She still wears brown, even though she's been with us for thousands of years. She has yet to earn her wings, Gabriel. Each task set for her has ended in disaster. Remember what happened to the Sphinx when she was sent to help that Pharaoh's daughter? My nose hurts even thinking about it. Do I even have to mention the Venus de Milo? She was supposed to inspire the boy to follow in his father's footsteps, but wound up almost destroying a great piece of art. I can't even hear a bell without seeing that huge crack. That happened just a few hundred years ago. She's still not ready. Not for something important."

Milicent stopped pacing as Gabriel stood to stand before her.

"I think she deserves another chance and I have faith in her abilities. Everyone deserves a second chance."

Milicent turned toward the door.

"Second chance? I think we're up to the sixth or seventh. Fine, if you insist, but never say I didn't warn you. I'll send her down immediately."

Gabriel smiled as the doors closed behind her. He wondered who would benefit most from this assignment, Emmeline or the girl? He hoped both.

$$*\qquad *\qquad *\qquad *$$

Megan watched the rain streaming down the bus window. The darkness carried her farther away from her home in Orlando. No, not her home. Her foster parents' home.

"The rain will stop before we get to New Orleans."

Megan jumped at the voice next to her.

"What did you say?"

"I said the rain will stop before we get to New Orleans." Emmeline looked at the timepiece that hung from her neck. "Actually, it will stop in twelve minutes, seventeen seconds to be precise."

Megan looked at the girl seated next to her. She looked about twelve, same as herself. She had long red hair and wore a brown tee shirt and jeans.

"Where'd you come from? I know was sitting alone."

Emmeline offered her hand to Megan as she introduced herself.

"You looked lonely, Megan, so I thought I'd keep you company. My name is Emmeline. It's nice to meet you."

Megan wondered if she was a runaway like herself.

"Wait, how'd you know my name? Who are you, anyway?"

"I told you, I'm Emmeline. I know your name because I'm an Angel and I've come to help you."

Megan rolled her eyes and turned to stare out the window again to avoid talking to the girl who thinks she's an Angel.

"You don't believe me do you? I guess I'll just have to prove it."

As Megan looked out the window, the rain turned to snow, but instead of falling down, it was falling up, toward the sky.

"Oh dear, I did it again. It's the atmospheric pressure. It's different here than it is in Heaven. I always miscalculate. I'll just turn it off. Hopefully, I've convinced you that I am an Angel."

The snow had turned to rain once again. Megan was still skeptical but was willing to talk to Emmeline.

"Okay, so you're an Angel. Who says I need help?"

Emmeline pulled two apples out of a pocket that Megan hadn't noticed earlier and handed her one.

"Oh, I don't know. Let's see, you're running away from your parents and traveling by yourself to a city where you don't know anyone. You don't have much money and no place to live once you get there. Yeah, you're right. You don't need any help."

Megan handed the apple back. She didn't need advice or apples.

"First of all, they're my 'foster' parents. I've been living with them for the past three years but they've never made a move to adopt me, and now they have a baby on the way and I'm sure they won't need me anymore. I have a friend in

New Orleans that I've been writing to in a chat room that will let me stay with her until I find a place of my own."

Emmeline handed the apple back to her.

"Do you know why an Angel was sent to you, Megan?"

"Beats me...I didn't ask for one, that's for sure."

Emmeline reached into her pocket once again and pulled out a large silver frame. In it was the family photo that hung on the wall of her foster parents' bedroom. Megan wondered how she got the picture, but wondered even more how she was able to fit it in her pocket.

"No, Megan, you didn't ask for an Angel. But they did. When your parents found you gone they prayed for your safe return. Gabriel heard them and had Milicent send me down to help you. I'll explain who they are later...they're sort of my 'foster' parents and even though I mess up a lot, they still love me, just like your parents still love you. Anyway, here I am. I've done some research on this case. It's always good to get all the facts before making any decisions or taking any action."

Megan reached for the picture and held it as Emmeline continued.

"Those people in that picture are your parents, and legally as of 2:00 p.m. yesterday. They just got permission two months ago to formally adopt you, even though they've been trying for years. Social services wanted to make sure there were no other relatives before finally allowing the adoption. They didn't say anything to you so that you wouldn't be disappointed if they were denied."

Tears glistened in Megan's eyes as she listened to Emmeline.

"But they have a kid of their own on the way, why would they still want me?"

Emmeline took the picture and placed it back in her pocket. Once again, it would be hanging on the wall at home.

"Maybe because they have enough love for both of you? What do you think?"

Megan closed her eyes and let the tears flow down her cheeks.

"I think I need a little more information before making anymore decisions. I'll start with Angels. Is it true that a bell rings when an Angel gets her wings?"

Emmeline blushed at this question and related the story of what happened the last time she rang a bell in celebration of one of her friends receiving her wings.

"You mean that's what caused the crack on the Liberty bell?"

Megan laughed at Emmeline's nod and then suddenly became serious again.

"I just realized that I don't have enough money to get back to Orlando."

Emmeline pointed to the window. The sign at the bus station read "Orlando". Megan could see her parents waiting for her on the curb.

"How'd you do that?"

She looked at the seat next to her, but it was empty.

A little brass bell that was hanging off the driver's rearview mirror started to ring. Megan watched it as she walked to the front of the bus. "Nah, it couldn't be, could it?" Suddenly, the bell cracked. Megan laughed. "I guess it could."

TIME IN A BOTTLE

CHAPTER ONE
Somewhere in the Atlantic Ocean—May 26, 1892

The ship groaned as it was tossed relentlessly upon the waves. The crew worked steadily to keep it afloat amidst the violent tirade of the whirling storm. Waves washed upon the deck and the strong winds ripped at the weakening sails. The Captain shouted orders to his men, grasping the wheel firmly as he steered, using instinct rather than sight to guide him through the storm. He'd sailed in rougher storms than this before and he knew he'd make it through this time too.

Vicky wasn't as hopeful as the Captain. Below deck, in her parents' cabin, she felt the ship sway back and forth. She wasn't certain if the queasiness in her stomach was more from fear or the sharp movements of the ship, or maybe a combination of the two. She looked over at the chair where her mother sat rocking her younger brother, John. She was sure the slight tinge of green in her mother's face mirrored her own, but her three year old brother seemed unaffected. In fact, he was actually sleeping.

She wished that her father would hurry back. He went up on deck to help when the storm first brewed and now, hours later, the storm was still in full force. Vicky left the bed where she had been sitting and moved over to where her mother sat, lowering herself to the floor to sit by her legs. She leaned her head on her mother's lap, finding a spot that wasn't occupied by John.

"Will it ever end, Mama? Is Papa okay up there?"

Her mother gently stroked her hair, only pausing for a brief moment when the ship began to lurch once again. "Don't worry, honey. Your papa will be okay.

The storm should be running its course soon. Just close your eyes and soon every-thing will be back to normal."

Vicky closed her eyes and tried to think of something other than the storm above. She knew that at the age of eleven she shouldn't be such a scaredy-cat, but even the adults on the ship looked anything but calm when they started tossing back and forth. She was sure that a lot of the other passengers were confined to their cabins, feeling the same way she was.

Her thoughts strayed to London, her home until recently. She already missed her friends that she left behind over a month ago dearly. They used to have such fun playing games together at Hyde Park and staying over at each other's house. Will she ever find friends like that when they get to America? Oh, why did her Papa have to take that transfer at his bank and make them move away from all that they were familiar with? He was so excited about going to a new land that Mama didn't have the heart to protest even though she'd be leaving her friends and family too.

Suddenly, the door burst open and her father stumbled in, swaying with the movement of the ship as he walked over to where they were sitting. His hair hung over his eyes and dripped water down his face. He removed the rain slick he wore, which apparently hadn't been very effective since his clothes were soaking wet. "I've never seen anything like it before. The waves are tremendous. I can't believe the ship is still upright." Looking at the faces of his wife and daughter as he made this pronouncement caused him to alter his next words. "Of course, we've gotten through the worst by now. The Captain seems to know what he's doing. He's a fine man. We'll be out of this storm before you know it."

His words became prophetic when, quite suddenly, the lurching stopped. The howling winds and noisy thunder ceased. Everything was now quiet. Jacob Tren-ton walked over to the porthole. Vicky stood up and ran across the cabin to stand by her father as they both looked out at the sea. It was calm again. Almost too calm. The ocean looked as if a sheet of ice covered it. Nothing stirred in the water or, as her eyes gazed up, in the sky either. The sun was disguised by a thick haze that seemed to surround the ship. None of the seagulls that she had so frequently seen during their voyage were anywhere to be found. Probably driven off by the storm, she thought.

"Papa, everything seems so still."

Her father took her hand and squeezed it gently. "Well, you've heard of the 'calm before the storm'. This must be the calm after the storm. All that really matters is that it's finally over. I'll go back up on deck and see if the Captain can tell us how far off course this storm took us today."

Vicky held onto her father's hand as he turned away from the window. "Can I go with you, papa?" He looked over at his wife and the slight nod of her head was all the encouragement he needed to give in to his daughter.

"I guess I see no reason why you shouldn't. It seems safe enough now." He nodded back at his wife who was still rocking their slumbering son. "We'll be right back then."

Vicky waited patiently for her father as he went into the water closet to change quickly into some dry clothes. As they exited the cabin, they noticed some of the other passengers venturing out of theirs, joining them as they followed the steps leading to the deck of the ship. She listened to the others talking about the storm, most of them relegating the woes of their spouses or children's 'mal de mer,' who they left behind to be close to the chamber pots.

Vicky's stomach became queasy once again as they ascended up the stairway. This time she knew it wasn't from the tossing ship. Something was wrong. There should've been crew members bustling all around carrying out their Captain's orders to set the ship right again. There were no crew, there was no Captain; there was only silence. Her father pulled her along as they walked the entire deck with the other passengers. Their worried mutterings filled her ears as she herself felt very frightened. One of the men walked over to her father, obviously outraged by their find. "This is incomprehensible. The entire crew and Captain deserting their passengers during a storm. This is intolerable…."

Jacob Trenton looked over at the life boats that still hung from the rig. "I don't think they did desert us. If they left the ship, it was without a boat. I was up on deck with them not five minutes before the storm ceased and they were all still up here."

Once again they walked the deck looking for someone or some clue as to the where-about of the ship's crew. There was a mixture of fear and anger among the passengers' faces. Another man approached Vicky's father. "You were up here with them, then tell us where they've gone. If they haven't deserted us, then what happened to them?"

Jacob Trenton could only shrug as he looked out at the still sea. Through the haze, he could see the outline of an island in the distance. "I don't know anymore than you do, but I do know that unless any of you know how to sail this ship, we need to make for land and soon, before another storm brews in. We'll have to take the life boats and row to that island over there. Someone is going to notice if the 'Wellesley' fails to make port eventually and send a search party. In the mean-time, we'll at least be on dry land."

CHAPTER TWO
An Island off the Coast of Nova Scotia—June 10, 1965

"Make sure you pick up all the driftwood and debris the storm blew onto my beach last night. If I'm going to be stuck with you this summer while your parents go gallivanting around Europe, you better make yourself useful."

Ginnie grabbed the handles of the wheel barrow that Aunt Vera pushed in front of her and began to roll it along the small stretch of sand behind her great aunt's beach house. She was staying with her mother's aunt while her parents were in Europe on business.

Her father's diplomatic duties took him from their home in Washington D.C. to several cities across the European continent to meet with other delegates. Her mother accompanied him, having the reputation of being a good hostess and a great dance partner for her dad at the various galas and functions they were required to attend. Since they would be too busy to spend much time with Ginnie during their travels, they asked Aunt Vera if Ginnie could stay with her for the summer. Aunt Vera had grudgingly agreed and constantly reminded Ginnie of what a burden she is for an old woman like herself to be responsible for.

After an hour of walking on the hot sand, Ginnie rolled the wheel barrow back into the tool shed and started sifting through the garbage she had picked up. She had a full load since there had been more than one bad storm in the past few weeks that hit the island hard with plenty of rain and wind. The sun today was a welcome sight.

The wood she piled in the corner along with the logs for Aunt Vera to use for burning in her fireplace. She threw the wrappers and other bits of debris into her Aunt's garbage can, along with a few empty soda bottles. As she was about to throw the last bottle into the bin, she stopped her arm in mid air and turned it over in her hands. It was an old wine bottle that had most of the label washed away. It looked like there was something inside it.

Ginnie walked out of the shed into the sunlight to get a better look at the bottle. She pulled the cork out and looked through the opening at the top. It looked like some kind of paper rolled up and lying at the bottom of it. "Don't tell me, someone put a message in a bottle. This is either some new form of advertising or some kind of joke. I'm sure it wasn't Aunt Vera. She wouldn't waste a perfectly good piece of paper, yet alone her time, to play a joke on anyone. Oooh, why did my parents have to stick me here this summer? Even summer camp would have been better than this."

She tipped the bottle over and the paper fell to the opening. Using the tips of two of her fingers, she was able to pry it out at last. She unrolled it a little bit and studied the curious handwriting before actually reading the note. It reminded her of the old English writing she had seen in one of her father's history books. Ginnie unraveled it all the way and began to read it.

Dear Friend,

Mama says that I must practice my letters even though we are far away from home and have no idea where we are. If you are reading this, then there is hope that we will find our way back as this bottle found its way to you. We have been on this island for almost three weeks now. Papa believes that someone will look for us soon. I pray he is right. Someone must realize by now that the 'Wellesley" is lost and try to find us. If someone does find this bottle, please help us.

Vicky Trenton

Ginnie read the letter three times before deciding what to do. This must be some kind of joke. Who gets stranded on an island these days with the coast guard and planes they have, able to search if anyone's boat goes missing? But still, if no one knew about it, they wouldn't be looking. As much as she dreaded doing it, she decided to show the note to Aunt Vera.

She shut the doors to the shed and took the bottle and letter with her into the house. She found Aunt Vera peeling potatoes in the kitchen. "Did you empty out the wheel barrow before putting it away?" Her aunt didn't even look up at her as she asked the question.

Ginnie tucked the letter in her pocket and placed the bottle on the counter as she reached for a glass and turned on the cold water tap. After drinking two glasses full, she washed her hands and moved over to Aunt Vera. She picked up a potato and grabbed a paring knife from the table.

"I emptied it and sorted everything before closing up the shed." Ginnie sat beside Aunt Vera at the table helping her peel potatoes for supper, contemplating the long summer ahead of her. It would be kind of neat if the bottle did come from someone stranded on an island. It would sure add a little excitement to her endless days with her great aunt. The days weren't only longer because it was summer, but also because Aunt Vera made them feel that way.

Vera tossed the last peeled potato into the pot and covered them with water before placing them on the stove. As she gathered up the peels into the bowl and placed them on the counter, she noticed the bottle that Ginnie had placed there. "What's this thing doing here on my clean counter? It looks like a dirty old bottle."

Ginnie stood up and pulled the note she found from her pocket and unrolled it to show her. "I found it on the beach this morning. It had this note inside it." Aunt Vera took the paper from her, a scowl forming on her face as she read it to herself.

"What a bunch of nonsense. Someone probably thinks this is funny. Throw it and the bottle away and run down to the village and get me some green beans from the grocer." Ginnie took back the paper and picked up the bottle. Aunt Vera handed her a dollar for the store. She went outside and walked back over to the shed where she threw the bottle away and closed the door again. She kept the letter. She didn't care what Aunt Vera said, she was not going to just shrug it off.

She decided to go to the library the next day and see if they have any information on any boats or ships that may have gone missing. They subscribed to a lot of the newspapers from the mainland across from the island; maybe one of them would mention something. What else did she have to do to alleviate the boredom?

The next morning, Ginnie grabbed an apple for her breakfast and ran out the back door before Aunt Vera could find more silly chores for her to do. "What did the old woman do before I came to stay?" Ginnie thought to herself. "I thought slavery had been abolished years ago. Of course that was in the states. Maybe Vera McKuen has started her own movement in the southern part of Canada. If that's the case, then I'm definitely rooting for the North."

She walked to the tiny village located on the island of Perdu where her Aunt lived. She arrived just as the library opened for the day. As she stepped inside, she looked for the area where the newspapers would be displayed. Though the library was a lot smaller than the one she visited in Washington, she still had trouble finding what she was looking for. She decided to ask the librarian for help.

The nameplate told her that she was standing in front of Mrs. Bridgeton. She waited until the woman finished stamping some cards before getting her attention. "Excuse me, ma'am, but I was wondering if you could help me?"

Mrs. Bridgeton looked up from her desk and smiled at Ginnie. "Oh, you must be the little girl staying with Vera this summer. Though I guess I shouldn't say little. You must be about eleven years old..."

"Actually, I'm twelve." Ginnie interrupted.

Mrs. Bridgeton nodded. "Oh yes, twelve. I was close then. I'm pretty good at guessing children's ages, especially when I see what kind of books they check out. Though in this small town where everyone pretty much knows everyone, you know each child from the moment they're born. Oh well, here I'm rambling and you look like you have a question."

"Yes ma'am, I was wondering where you keep the local newspapers; in particular, I'm looking for ones from the past few weeks through today."

Mrs. Bridgeton came from around the desk and motioned for Ginnie to follow her toward the back of the library. "We keep them for a month back here by the tables so people can come in and sit and read them at their leisure. After a month, we move them into the archives and file them away by date. Was there anything in particular you were looking for?"

Ginnie pulled the piece of paper she had from her pocket and read the name of the ship once again. "Actually, I was hoping to find any information there might be in the papers of any boats or ships that may have gone missing. The one I'm interested in is the Wellesley."

The librarian stopped in her tracks and turned around to face her. "If you're looking for information on the Wellesley, you'll need to look farther back than the past few weeks. The Wellesley was lost at sea over seventy years ago."

Ginnie looked back down at the paper in her hand, once again reading the name of the ship that Vicky Trenton wrote on it. "There must be another ship with the same name. The one I'm looking for would've been stranded in the past month or so."

Mrs. Bridgeton shook her head. "I haven't heard of any. No one else would want to use that name on their boat. Not when the original had such a tragic ending."

Ginnie was confused now. Maybe this whole thing was a joke after all. What did she really know about Canadians and their sense of humor?…but still, her gut instinct told her that there was something more to this. "What do you mean by a tragic ending? What happened to the Wellesley?"

Mrs. Bridgeton led her over to a table in the corner and bade her to sit while she walked over to the stacks and picked up a large scrapbook and brought it over to her. "Here, this should help explain. It holds all the newspaper clippings pertaining to the Wellesley. The lady who was the librarian at the time put it together since it made the headlines for several weeks and a brother of hers had been a passenger on the ship.

It appears that the ship that sailed from England, traveling to New York City, never made it to port. It was very strange though. The ship's captain and crew were found alive on a shore off the mainland across the way from our island here. That's probably why it made such news because most of the people who live on this island today are originally from the mainland. Their families were all living over there at the time the Wellesley was reported missing. The crew had no recollection of how they got there. There were no row boats and the ship was nowhere to be seen. Neither were the passengers."

The librarian left Ginnie alone to read the newspaper articles while she returned to her duties at her desk. Mrs. Bridgeton didn't seem to be the least bit curious as to why she was interested about this lost ship and she wasn't volunteering anything. What would she say? "I found a note in a bottle from a girl who claims to be a passenger on a ship that disappeared over seventy years ago." What if it took that many years for someone to finally find it? It's hard to believe that it would have been floating out there all this time, but the alternative was even harder to believe.

She opened the book and started reading all the clippings. By the time she was finished an hour and a half later, she was even more baffled than before she started. According to the articles, the ship left London and two months later the crew had been found, but not the ship, nor the passengers. The Captain told of the ferocious storm they had sailed through and that just when it was finally calm again and they were getting ready to check their course, he blacked out. When he came awake again, it was two months later and he was on an island with the rest of his crew who apparently had suffered the same malady. There was no sign of the ship or of how they even arrived there.

At first he thought that there had been mischief among the passengers and some of them had knocked them out and left them behind. However, he and the crew were alone in that theory. No one believed them; especially when months went by and no sign of the ship or its passengers had ever been found. It was assumed that the crew jumped ship during the storm and left the passengers to fend for themselves. No charges were ever brought forth since they had no substantial proof, though some thought the missing ship and passengers proof enough. But the scandal hung over them for the rest of their days as they lost the respect of their friends and family.

At the back of the album was a list of names of the passengers and crew members who had set sail on the Wellesley. There was a Jacob Trenton listed, traveling with wife and two children. Could Vicky have been one of his children? Ginnie briefly scanned the list of the crew members when one name caught her eye, *Arthur McKuen*. That's Aunt Vera's last name. I wonder if they could be related. Aunt Vera was in her early sixties, this happened over seventy years ago, before she was born. Could it be a great uncle or even her grandfather? She would've liked to have asked her, but considering the scandal that was involved, she didn't think Aunt Vera would appreciate her bringing it up. She didn't need her scowling at her any more than she did already.

She thought maybe she could ask her mother the next time she talked to her, since Vera was her aunt she'd probably know. But it would be kind of hard to bring up a subject like that long distance and especially if Aunt Vera was in ear shot of the phone conversation at the time.

Ginnie came to the conclusion that the bottle had been floating in the sea for all those years and debated if she should tell someone, like the newspaper or the Historical society. She was afraid to bring any attention to her though. She didn't think Aunt Vera would be too happy about it. When she got back to her Aunt's house, she went to the shed to retrieve the bottle before the bins were set out for the garbage truck the following day. She thought about holding onto it but then decided to send a note of her own across the sea. Maybe it would find its way to some other part of the world. Hopefully, it wouldn't take seventy years.

She went into the house and tip toed past the living-room where her Aunt was sitting in her chair taking an afternoon nap. She went up to her room and pulled out a piece of paper from a notebook she had brought with her and began to write.

Dear Friend,

I found a note in this bottle and decided to send one of my own. My name is Ginnie, I'm twelve years old, and spending the summer with my great Aunt on an island called Perdu in Nova Scotia, Canada. It's only been a week but feels like it's been a year. Aunt Vera isn't much fun. I hope who-ever finds this will write something too and toss it to the sea. Who knows how far this bottle can travel? It had come a long way when I finally found it.

Virginia (Ginnie) Maitlin

Ginnie rolled the piece of paper up and tucked it into the bottle, pushing the cork in real tight. She went back down the stairs quietly and out the back door. She walked to the beach and stood in front of the pounding waves. She lifted her arm that held the bottle high over her head and tossed it with all her might into the water. She stood there for a few minutes watching the bottle disappear before returning back to the house.

CHAPTER THREE
June 25, 1892

Vicky pretended to be asleep as she lay next to her little brother on the blankets spread out on the sand. She could hear her father talking with some of the other men. One man in particular with a loud voice seemed to ramble on.

"We can't stay here forever. It's been almost a month since we were stranded on this island. I don't think anyone is coming to look for us. I say we pull our resources and sail the ship back ourselves. Some of us have some knowledge in sailing. We should be able to set a course for port. It's very unnerving staring at that ship anchored out there in the ocean. It's almost taunting us"

Jacob Trenton couldn't blame the others for how they were feeling. He himself was ready to rejoin civilization. Their food rations would have ran out long ago if it hadn't been for the fish they were able to catch and the cocoanuts that grew on the island. Forty other people were with him and his family. The only ones who seemed to be adapting were the children who loved playing in the water and on the sand. But even they needed to get back to a rigid routine. Playtime had its limits and too much of it was not always a good thing. He looked over at where his own children were sleeping and smiled.

He waited his turn to speak and then offered his thoughts. "I agree. Just sitting here isn't getting us anywhere. But before we start sailing anywhere, we need to try and find our bearings and study the maps that the Captain had on board. Hopefully we should be able to figure out where we were before the storm hit and try to get back on track. I've tried using the compass I had with me when we sailed but it's useless. The needle keeps spinning and won't give me a direction. We should try the Captain's compass in his cabin. It may be more accurate. Why don't we all get a good night's sleep and some of us can row out to the ship in the morning and gather the things we'll need."

The other men nodded as they stood up and rejoined their families. They all kept close together around the huge campfire that they continued to feed with drift wood and anything else on the island that they could find that would burn. They hoped that some passing ship would spot it and rescue them.

*   *   *   *

The next morning, Vicky watched as her father rowed off toward the ship with some of the other men. After helping her mother and the other women prepare a breakfast of fruit and some of the last oatmeal they had left from the ship, she decided to take a walk.

She never thought she'd miss the taste of milk so much. The only thing she'd had to drink in the past month was water from a little pond they discovered on the other side of the island. It always had a fishy taste to it but you got used to it, especially when the hot afternoon sun made it sweltering. The hardest thing was filling buckets and any other containers that they could find that could hold water and trudging back with it to this side of the island. When she asked her father why they just didn't move their camp closer to the water, he told her they wanted to stay in sight of the ship.

After watching the row boat move out farther, she turned away and walked along the beach. The sand was soft beneath her bare feet. The heat of the day would drive most of the women under makeshift tents, but after the sun went down it could become quite cool in the evenings. That was when the fire was nice to have. She loved sitting around it with the other people, listening to them talk of their families and their homes.

It was quite beautiful here. Under different circumstances, she wouldn't mind living here if she had a house with four walls and a roof and some clean clothes to change into. And milk, plenty of milk would be nice. A few cows, and maybe some chickens for fresh eggs in the morning and some roasted chicken at night. Vicky sighed, just thinking about things that people normally took for granted.

She followed the sand until she found the spot where huge rocks created a little pool that they used to bath in since the water was a little calmer and it was easier for the little children. There was no one there at the moment so she sat down and dangled her feet in the water.

While deep in thought, she was surprised by a nudge on her shoulder. She turned her head to see her little brother John standing there holding his little stuffed bear and frowning at her.

"Johnny, what are you doing here? You're not supposed to walk off by yourself." Her little brother stuck his thumb in his mouth, then thought better of it since it was all sandy and climbed onto Vicky's lap.

"Icky don't play with me no more or tell me stories."

She tucked her little brother onto her lap better and gave him a kiss on the cheek.

"Icky is very sorry and will be happy when you can start pronouncing your v's. I guess everyone is out of sorts these days being stuck here. I promise to play with you later but how about if we just have a story now?" She assumed her brother's nodding head showed approval so she began her tale.

"Once upon a time there was a little boy who was very brave…"

Her brother lifted his head to look up at her. "Was his name John?" Vicky tucked the little bear in his arms and continued with the story.

"Yes his name was John but everyone called him Johnny. Now let me continue my story. Anyway, there was a brave little boy who was sailing on a boat all by himself. He fought fierce storms and even gigantic sea serpents until one day he landed on a shore of an island and decided to stay for awhile because he was tired of sailing so much. He wished that someone would sail by and find him because he really didn't like being alone and he didn't think his boat could stand much more punishment from the sea even if he did try sailing off once again."

"One day he found an old bottle that someone must have left on the island a long time ago. It was half buried in the sand and he pulled it out and decided to write a note and put it in the bottle…"

Johnny interrupted once again. "But I don't know how to write."

Vicky hugged her brother and then hushed him. "This Johnny knew how to write just like you will someday soon. Anyway, back to the story. He looked in his bag that he carried all his possessions in and found an old book that he'd read many times already…and before you say you can't read yet, this Johnny could read. He tore out a piece of paper from the back of the book and found a pencil tucked away in the bottom of the bag. He wrote a message telling whoever would find it that he was lost and alone and to please send someone to find him."

"He put the message in the bottle and sealed it and threw it out into the ocean as far as he could. A few days later, the bottle came back to him and in it was an answer to his letter. He pulled the note out of the bottle and rejoiced when he read the words that would save him. The message read:

> Dear Lonely Boy,
> Build a fire as high as the sky,
> And we will look for it morning and nigh.

And it was signed 'A friend'. So he built a fire and kept adding wood and leaves and anything he could find to keep it burning. He even burned his boat to make the fire burn higher and longer. Five days went by and one morning he looked out at the sea to discover a ship nearing the shore. The little boy was no longer lost and no longer alone."

Vicky looked down at her little brother who had fallen asleep in her arms. Her mother, who she hadn't noticed until now, was sitting behind them in the sand.

"That was a lovely story Vicky. I'm sure he'll like to hear it again when he awakens. Here, hand him over to me and I'll lay him down on his blanket."

Her mother bent over to pick up her brother from her arms and carried him back to their camp. Vicky remained sitting there with her legs in the water and admiring the day.

As she looked around, she saw something glistening in the sun that appeared to be stuck in some reeds. She stood up in the knee deep water and waded over to the spot, lifting her dress high enough without getting it wet or revealing too much of herself to the sun or anyone who came upon her.

As she got closer, she recognized the wine bottle she had thrown in the ocean a couple of weeks before. Disappointedly she picked it up out of the water. It must have gotten stuck in these plants and never made it out to sea. She carried it back over to where she was sitting and sat down on the sand, stretching her wet legs out in front of her to dry in the sun. She pulled the cork out of the bottle and removed the paper from inside. Right away she noticed it was a different paper from what she had put in. She had used a piece of her mother's stationary. This paper was thinner, with lines and looked like it had been torn from a book of some sort. Maybe the story she had told her little brother wasn't make-believe after all.

She unfolded the note and was ecstatic as she read the note that Ginnie had written. "Oh, I must show Papa when he gets back." Someone out there does know now that we are on this Island...but no sooner did that thought cross her mind that another thought as well. She knows we are on *an* island. But there is no way she could know which island. But at least someone knew they were still alive.

That afternoon she waited impatiently for her father to return from the ship. She had already shown her mother the note from the bottle. The sadness she had seen so often in her mother's eyes these past weeks had been replaced with a sign of hope. "Let us not say anything to the other women until you've spoken to your father. They have suffered enough disappointment already since we were forced to come ashore."

So Vicky obeyed her mother and awaited the return of Jacob Trenton. While she waited she reread the note a few times just too make sure she wasn't imagining it. "Virginia Maitlin, what a pretty name. I wonder if she's from England too. It doesn't matter really. I wonder if she's told others already too and if they are already looking for us now."

She was just dozing off when suddenly her eyes opened wide as she saw the row boat heading back to the island. She stood up and ran over to the water, watching her father and the other men as they jumped out of the boat and pulled it onto the sand. She waited for the other men to wander over to their families before approaching her father. He smiled as she ran up to him. One hand held a leather pouch that she assumed contained the maps. With his free hand, he reached down and tugged on her braid. "So what mischief have you been up to while I was gone?"

Vicky pulled the note from her pocket and handed it to him. "Papa, you have to read this. I wrote a letter and put it in a bottle and tossed it out to the sea. I didn't really expect to get a reply but Mama says that I still need to practice my writing while we are stuck here so I wrote a letter and on a whim sent it off in a bottle into the ocean. Today I found the bottle again and it wasn't my note in it but another girl's. She must've found my message and decided to do the same. Doesn't this mean that someone knows that we are still alive and maybe will come looking for us soon?

Her father unfolded the note and read it. "Vicky, dear, this was written by a child. Someone not much older than you and doesn't say any mention of our predicament. We can't even be sure she has shown your letter to anyone else."

At the look of his daughter's downtrodden face, he softened his words. "However, it just could be possible that she did. And, I assume that my smart daughter mentioned the name of our ship in her letter..." Vicky nodded as her father paused. "I'm sure that if she lives somewhere in the vicinity of where our journey was taking us originally, ahh let's see," he scanned the note once again; "aah yes, she does say Nova Scotia which I believe is not too far from the States and New York is close to Canada. She may have heard some news of the missing "Wellesley', and may have done just what you did and showed it to her Papa.

"We'll show this piece of paper to the others around the fire tonight and see what they think about it. In the meantime, I need to find a quiet spot where I can study these maps. I'm afraid the compass on the ship wasn't working accurately either and I'm going to try and figure out just how far the storm caused us to veer off from our original course." He leaned down and kissed Vicky on the cheek before walking away.

CHAPTER FOUR
July 11, 1965

Ginnie stared up at the ceiling in her room. She already counted the number of rose buds on the wallpaper trim and now she was watching a spider as it spun a web while it dangled from the light fixture. At least the spider wasn't bored. She could hear her Aunt move around in the kitchen downstairs. Soon she would be calling for her to get up.

She decided to beat her to the punch and threw the covers off and slowly rose from the bed. She had taken a bath the night before after talking to her parents for a few minutes when they phoned from Paris. Still, she trudged to the bathroom to fulfill a very necessary function at that moment and then splash some water on her face and brush her teeth. She looked up at the mirror on the medicine cabinet and stuck her tongue out at herself. She didn't like the freckles that were popping out all over her cheeks from the sun. Her brown hair had strands of blond that had been bleached by the hours she spent out in the sun. Her mother had to pay twenty dollars at her hair salon to get her blond streaks.

"Who would want to be in Paris when they could be here with Aunt Vera? She's sturdier than the Eiffel Tower and older than the Arch de Triomphe. Okay, maybe not that old."

Ginnie walked back to her room a little less groggy and a bit more revived from the water on her face. She dressed in cotton shorts and a tee shirt and went downstairs to join Aunt Vera in the kitchen. When she reached the bottom step, she stopped short. Aunt Vera was lying on the floor by the refrigerator, her eyes closed and her face pale.

"Aunt Vera, are you okay? She rushed over to her and knelt down beside her. She could see her chest rise and fall and knew a great sense of relief that she was still breathing. She rushed to the phone and called the local sheriff's office for help.

$$* \qquad * \qquad * \qquad *$$

Someone tapped Ginnie's shoulder, nudging her awake as she sat up on the bench that she had fallen asleep on. She looked up and saw Mrs. Bridgeton smiling down at her, concern showing in her eyes. She looked toward the window and could see that night had already fallen.

"Mrs. Bridgeton, what are you doing here? What time is it? How's Aunt Vera doing?"

The librarian sat down next to her and put her arm around Ginnie. "One question at a time dear. First of all, Vera is doing fine. She must've forgotten to take her blood pressure medicine, though if I know Vera, she probably just decided she didn't want to take it and her blood pressure shot up and caused her to faint. I'm so glad you were there to find her before it was too late. The time is nine o'clock and that's why I'm here. They're going to keep your Aunt here for a couple of days to run some tests and keep her under observation and I'm here to take you home with me until she gets released. But first we need to get some food in you. Have you had anything at all to eat yet today?"

Ginnie stood up and stretched the kinks from her neck and back. Sleeping on a hospital bench was definitely not good for one's posture. "I had a peanut butter sandwich in the cafeteria around noon, but that's about it. I'd like to visit Aunt Vera if I could. You don't have to take me home with you, I'll be alright at Aunt Vera's by myself."

Mrs. Bridgeton grabbed her purse from the seat and motioned for Ginnie to follow her down the hall toward the hospital exit. "It's past visiting hours and they don't usually let children come into the rooms, but we'll see what we can do tomorrow. Aunt Vera is already asleep for the night anyway. I just left her a few minutes ago. You are not going to stay by yourself in that house. We'll stop there on the way to my place and get some clean clothes for you and your toothbrush. Vera and I go way back and I have plenty of room since all my kids have grown and left home and my husband died five years ago. I just live down the road from Vera, so you'll still be close to the house. Now come on and when we get to my house, I'll fix you a nice sandwich, turkey, not peanut butter, before you go to bed."

*   *   *   *

When Ginnie woke up the next morning, she couldn't figure out where she was at first. Instead of rose buds on the wall paper trim there were lilacs, and the bed she was lying in had a white coverlet instead of the pink one that she usually had. When memory returned and she realized she was at Mrs. Bridgeton's house, she felt shy. She didn't know this woman very well though she seemed to be a nice lady, she felt uncomfortable making herself at home here. Then it occurred to her that she never felt comfortable at Aunt Vera's either, which made her feel less embarrassed as she got up and made her way to the bathroom.

As she entered the bathroom, she saw that Mrs. Bridgeton had laid out a fresh towel and wash cloth by the sink for her. She quickly washed and got dressed and left the room she was staying in to search out the librarian. She found her by the stove in the kitchen making pancakes. Mrs. Bridgeton turned her head toward her direction when she walked in. "I was just going to wake you. I thought you might like some pancakes for breakfast."

Ginnie sat down at one of the two place settings at the small round table in the corner by the window. "That's great, Mrs. Bridgeton. I'm starving." The lady flipped the last pancake onto a large platter and shut off the stove before joining Ginnie at the table.

"Here you go dear, eat up. And no more Mrs. Bridgeton now. You can call me Maggie. When you're finished, we can call the hospital and see if you can visit Vera today."

Ginnie grabbed a pancake and plopped it on her plate, slathering it with maple syrup. "Thanks Mrs...I mean Maggie. I hope I'm not keeping you from the library today."

Maggie placed some of the pancakes on her own plate and reached for the syrup. "I'm off on Saturdays. We have college students that work part-time on the weekends so that us old duffers can rest up. So did you sleep well?"

"Yeah, that bed is a lot more comfortable than the bench at the hospital. I really appreciate your letting me stay here. I guess I should contact my parents and let them know what happened, but I'm not really sure how to reach them in Paris."

Maggie placed another pancake on Ginnie's plate. "Eat up dear, you didn't eat much yesterday. Don't worry your folks right now. Vera is doing fine and I'm sure the tests are just routine. If anything should develop, we'll make sure they know. In the meantime, you're welcome here for as long as you like."

Ginnie gobbled down the last bite of pancake wishing she could stay here and not go back to Aunt Vera's. Oh well, time to visit the dragon. No sooner did the thought enter her mind that she already regretted it. Aunt Vera really wasn't a dragon. No matter what, she was still family. She remembered seeing her on the kitchen floor the other day and how scared she was when she thought Aunt Vera was dying.

Later that morning, Maggie was able to sneak Ginnie in to see Aunt Vera as long as she didn't stay too long. Aunt Vera was sipping a cup of tea when they entered the room.

"How ya feeling, Aunt Vera?"

"How do you expect I'd be feeling?" She paused when she looked over at Maggie and Ginnie noticed a look that passed between the two women that she couldn't read. It was almost like Maggie was staring her down. It must've worked because when Aunt Vera continued to talk again, she spoke much softer. "I'm feeling fine considering that yesterday morning I was out cold on the floor." She looked over at Ginnie and she could swear that she saw a slight smile form on Aunt Vera's mouth. "Thanks to you dear, for calling for help. I'm sorry I haven't been much fun this summer. I guess I'm just used to being alone. We'll make up for it when I get home."

That afternoon, when they returned to Maggie's house, Ginnie was still reeling from Aunt Vera's change of heart. She helped Maggie bake Chocolate Chip cookies and afterward they sat down at the table and enjoyed some of them while they were still warm. Maggie interrupted her thoughts when she spoke to her.

"I know what you're thinking, dear, that your Aunt Vera must be sicker than you thought to suddenly change her mood so fast. She really isn't always like the way you've seen her this summer. I have been friends with that woman for many years and she does have a good heart. I think that she just gets lonely sometimes by herself, but also isn't used to having anyone around either, especially children."

"She never did marry and have a family, and just experiencing these past five years alone since my husband died helps me to understand the loneliness she must feel at times. I at least still have my children and grandchildren that come to visit me from time to time. I think that I'm going to take a nap before starting supper. Why don't you look over the books I have in the study and pick one you like and sit out on the beach and have a good read."

Ginnie helped her clear up the dishes from their afternoon snack and followed Maggie to her study. After showing her the room, Maggie went off in the direction of her bedroom. Ginnie looked at all the books that lined the shelves on all four walls. Even the windows had shelves underneath them that held paperbacks.

She scanned the titles and decided on a Charles Dickens' novel, 'A Christmas Carol'. It would probably appear strange to read a Christmas book in July, but why not? She always wanted to read Dickens and she enjoyed the movie she once saw on television. A few days ago she would've said that Scrooge and her Aunt had a lot in common. But since that morning in her hospital room together with what Maggie told her made her see Aunt Vera in a different light.

She decided to walk over to her Aunt's house and sit out by the beach while she read. After a couple of hours, she figured it was time to head back and help Maggie with supper. She walked along the beach behind the house and made a mental note to come back the next day and pick up some of the drift wood that the tide washed in before Aunt Vera came home.

She opened her book and continued reading as she walked by the water. She stopped when she hit something with her toe. A bottle was laying half buried in the sand. She bent down to retrieve it, wondering if it was the same one she found before. "Well jeepers, how do ya like that? I can't even get a bottle to float out to sea. It must've washed back up on shore right after I tossed it in. Oh well, I'll just carry it back to the shed and toss it in the bin." She opened the bottle to pull out the letter she had written.

As soon as she got the piece of paper out, she knew it wasn't the one from her notebook. "Well, this is strange. I wonder how many notes in a bottle are floating around in the sea anyway? I guess it's a good way to save on postage, but probably not too reliable." She unfolded the paper and realized it was from the same girl who had written before. Ginnie sat down on the sand, her brain trying to process what her eyes were seeing.

"Alright, now I can see some bottle floating in the water for years until some-one finally finds it, but how can this bottle have an answer from my letter from a girl who supposedly wrote it over seventy years ago? Someone is definitely playing some kind of weird game here. She looked down at the note in her hand and reread what Vicky had written.

Dear Friend,

This bottle does not need a ship to travel across the sea. It found its way to you. I hope it finds you once again. I wish we could follow it home. If it is you Virginia, who reads this, know that we are grateful to realize we have someone out there who knows we are here and gives us hope that we will soon be found. We stare at the Wellesley from the shore of this island and wonder about the crew's fate and our own. It is now the twelfth day of July, 1892. Hopefully, you receive this message once again before the year grows much older and I run out of stories to tell my little brother. My papa is trying to find this island on the maps from the ship, but has not had any luck so far. I hope another ship follows this magical bottle that seems to know the way and sets us free.

Your friend,

Vicky Trenton

Ginnie rolled up the letter and pushed it back into the bottle. She decided to return to Aunt Vera's to pick something up before returning to Maggie's. When she arrived at the house, she ran inside and up the stairs to her bedroom. She opened the bottom drawer of the dresser and found the previous note she had tucked away as a keepsake. She grabbed it and shut the drawer and ran back downstairs and back to Maggie's.

Maggie was cooking hamburgers in a frying pan on the stove when Ginnie walked in. "Oh there you are honey, I was just going to call for you. How about some corn on the cob with the burgers?"

Ginnie put the bottle down on the floor by the kitchen door and walked over to the sink to wash her hands. "That sounds great Maggie, can I help with something?"

Maggie threw four corn cobs into a pot of boiling water and nodded toward the table. "You can lay the place settings if you'd like. The plates are in the cupboard over the sink and the silverware in that drawer behind you."

Ginnie busied herself with the dishes and laying the forks and knives on the linen napkins that Maggie used. She was stalling for time before showing the notes and the bottle to Maggie, wondering if she'd think she was being silly. She had just finished filling two glasses with water when Maggie put down a platter of burgers and a bowl with the corn on the cobs on the table and they began to eat.

After they finished, Ginnie stood to clear the plates. Maggie refrained her by placing a hand on her arm. "That's okay dear, we can take care of that after you show me the bottle you brought back with you."

Ginnie's mouth fell open and she closed it again as she sat back down in her chair. Maggie smiled at her as she leaned over and picked up the bottle from the floor. "Don't be so surprised. Being a librarian for thirty years, I've grown eyes on the back of my head to keep watch over some of the little hooligans that come into my library. Now this looks like an old empty wine bottle and I have a feeling you brought it here to show it to me, am I correct?"

Ginnie recovered her voice and nodded as she answered her. "Yes. I thought of showing you what I found but then I thought that maybe you would think it was all just a big joke and I was being silly."

Maggie looked at the bottle and then placed it on the table in front of her. "First of all, I would never think of anything that you seem to be very serious about silly. Second of all, why don't you just go ahead and ask?"

"Ok, well, you remember that day I came to see you in the library, I asked about the Wellesley. The reason I had asked was because I had found this bottle on the sand when I was cleaning up a lot of the debris that washed up on Aunt

Vera's beach after that big storm we had earlier. In the bottle was this note." Ginnie pulled out both notes from her pocket and unfolded them to show her the right one. She handed it to Maggie and waited while she read it.

Maggie's brow furrowed as she read and then she looked up at Ginnie. "You say that this was in the bottle?" Ginnie nodded and then handed her the other note.

"After you told me that the Wellesley was lost over seventy years ago, I just assumed that this Vicky Trenton wrote it that long ago, and it just washed ashore finally last month. Just for the heck of it, I wrote my own 'message in the bottle' so to speak, not really seriously thinking it would wind up anywhere. Today, I was walking on the beach by Aunt Vera's and I stubbed my toe on something buried halfway in the sand. It was this bottle. I thought that it just washed back on shore right away, but when I opened it up and pulled out the note, it was another one from this girl answering my letter. Tell me what you think. Do you think someone's playing a joke?"

Maggie read both letters again and then looked at the wine bottle. "This is an old bottle but I guess someone could have had it tucked away in the attic somewhere along with this stationary. But, I just can't imagine anyone around here joking about something pertaining to the Wellesley. Wait here a minute."

Maggie stood up and went into the study and brought a photo album similar to the one she had seen at the library. "My family kept their own copies of the newspaper articles about the incident. I had an uncle that was on the crew and my mother's family was frantic those two months they were missing. You know, the whole circumstances surrounding that voyage were peculiar, and no one believed the crew when they said they didn't know what happened and swore they didn't abandon the passengers. No one except those few like my mother and my grandmother who knew my uncle would never have participated in anything like that."

Ginnie turned the pages in the book, reading over again what she had read at the library. "Here's the name of Trenton that I'd seen when I looked at the one in the library. Vicky signs her last name as Trenton. See here on the passenger list. It mentions Jacob Trenton and wife and two children. Vicky could be one of the children." She hesitated before asking the next question. "Maggie, I see that one of the crew had a last name of McKuen. Do you know if he's related to Aunt Vera?"

Maggie moved her seat closer to Ginnie as they looked at the album together. "I believe that was her grandfather. Vera was born ten years after the incident and she never got to know him. They say he took a boat out to sea one day to look for the lost ship and was never seen again."

"It affected Vera through her father who was heartbroken and was never the same again. It's most likely because of it that Vera built that invisible wall around her that's lonelier than the house she lives in on this island. I think the name *Perdu* is what attracted her to this place. It means 'lost' in French and is a fairly new community."

"Someone sailing on his yacht about thirty years ago supposedly got lost out here and this was where he wound up. He was discovered a few days later and decided to buy the island and named it Perdu. There are a lot of people in Canada who speak both French and English, he thought the name appropriate. So did a lot of other people from the Mainland who saw the irony in another ship being lost in these waters."

"A lot of them decided to move their families out here after the village was starting to take shape with new houses being built and he even built a school house for any children that came to the island. Some of the men are fishermen who work off the island. Some of the others are businessmen who commute back and forth each day on the ferry and some are just retired folks and looking for a place to get away from the hustle and bustle of the everyday world. Oh well, listen to me. I'm rambling on again."

They both continued to scan the clippings, trying to find something to help them piece together this puzzle. "Maggie, do you think this is possible? That this girl really is Vicky Trenton who set sail with her family seventy years ago and is writing to me from the past? How can that be?"

"I've read enough books and seen enough things in my sixty-two years to believe anything is possible. H.G. Wells would think it was possible."

"Who?"

Maggie rolled her eyes. "What have you been reading dear? H.G. Wells was a great writer. Don't tell me you've never read any of his books?" Ginnie shook her head but showed her the book she had been reading today. "No, but I did find this book by Charles Dickens in your study and started reading it today. I'm really enjoying it. But I had heard of Dickens before. Who is H.G. Wells?"

"H. G. Wells was a great writer. He wrote a book called 'The Time Machine' that would definitely make sense in this situation. There's a copy at the library you can borrow. One could sit in the time machine and travel to any place in time either in the past or the future. I know it's just fiction but it's almost like the bottle itself is a time machine carrying your letters back and forth not only across the water, but across time."

Ginnie's mind mulled over what Maggie just said. Growing up in a home in Washington, D.C. where one always thought inside the box, it was strange to suddenly think outside it. To stretch the imagination beyond what one can see and believe in something that you can't.

"I wish that we could locate this island that they are stranded on and I could write her again and give them their location. They could follow the maps that they must have if they had some point of reference to go by."

Maggie looked deep in thought as she stood up and started to clear the dishes off the table. She filled the sink with water and dish soap and began to wash and rinse the dishes. Ginnie got up and grabbed a dish towel and almost dropped the plate she picked up from the rack when Maggie suddenly spoke.

"I've got it! It may be a long shot, but I have copies of old maps from the past one hundred years in the library. If you really believe that this girl is real, we can go through the maps that would be accurate for that time period and compare them with today's maps and maybe we'll find an island on a current map that didn't show up seventy years ago because no one knew it existed yet."

"Maggie, I think I do believe she's really writing me and I think that you do too. But what I want to know is if you think that Aunt Vera will."

CHAPTER FIVE
July 12, 1892

Vicky sat on the beach, watching the stars above light up the evening sky. She could hear the other people a few yards behind her talking, as they threw more wood into the fire and drank the last of the tea that came from the ship. They seemed a little more cheerful and hopeful after Vicky's father showed them the note she found in the bottle. They decided to wait a little longer for a rescue ship to find them.

She had written another letter and placed it in the bottle like she had done once before, throwing it out into the sea in the same place as last time. She wanted to make sure she did everything the same so as not to disturb whatever magic spell may have been cast on that precious bottle. Her father moved from the others and sat down beside her on the sand.

"It was only a few hours ago since you tossed it back into the water. I don't think you need to stand watch all night. We don't even know if it will wind up in the same place again or anywhere at all this time."

Vicky leaned her head on her father's shoulder. I am not standing watch, I'm sitting. I know that I won't see anything tonight, Papa. I just thought that if I sat here long enough, that maybe my thoughts or prayers will help guide it along. I know it sounds crazy, Papa. But I do believe someone out there is trying to help us right now." Vicky yawned as her eyes closed and a few minutes later she did not waken as her father carried her to the blanket and tucked her into bed next to her brother John.

*   *   *   *

The next morning Vicky awakened to overcast skies. It looked like a bad storm was moving in. They had a few rain showers that didn't last long in the past few weeks, but the skies had never looked this dark before, at least not since the terrible storm that they had sailed through on the ship.

After breakfast, her father went with some of the other men to look for better shelter from the inevitable storm. While they were gone, she helped her mother and the other ladies pack up the blankets and makeshift tents and other items that they had brought from the ship for easy transport later when they had to move camp. They still kept the fire going strong, even though they knew that eventually, if the storm brought heavy rains, it would probably go out. But until then, they let it blaze.

Her brother John stood by her at the fire as she threw some tree branches into it, throwing some leaves of his own to add to the fire.

"Don't stand too close, Johnny, I don't want you to get burned. Here let's just throw the rest of these branches in and then we'll go over there and I'll help you build a sand castle."

They tossed in the last of the leaves and moved away from the fire. When Vicky sat down on the sand, she reached out for her little brother to join her but he shook his head at her. "Don't want to play sand, want to go play in water with Icky."

As she stood back up, Vicky looked up at the sky and watched a few of the sea gulls scattering among the darkening clouds. She looked down at the ocean, and noticed the tides were a little choppier today than they had been.

"The water is a bit rough today, Johnny, and I don't think we should venture too far from camp right now to go to the pool. I know. How about this? If it looks likes it's clearing up by this afternoon, I'll take you to the pool so you can wade it in for a little while."

She thought to herself that even if it didn't clear up, which was the more likely possibility, she would still make a hurried trip to the pool and see if she would find her bottle again in the same spot as before. She really hoped that an answer would come soon. It looked like they were running out of time. If the storm was bad enough, they could lose the ship completely, and there would be no way of getting home unless someone found them.

She took her brother by the hand and led him over to a tree and motioned for him to sit down next to her in the sand under it. She grabbed a small twig and started drawing lines criss cross in the sand. "How about if we play a game of noughts and crosses? You can choose if you want to be X or O."

Once again her brother shook his head at her. "Tell me story!"

Vicky looked up at the sky silently praying that someone out there was trying to find them. "I was afraid that you were going to say that."

CHAPTER SIX
July 13, 1965

Ginnie woke up early while the sun was just peeking out from the sky. Instead of laying there and counting the spots on the ceiling, for once she had a new ambition. The recent boredom she was experiencing had been replaced with a challenge that she was committed to.

With this new goal ahead of her, she jumped out of bed and made a bee line for the bathroom. She could hear Maggie downstairs already in the kitchen as she finished brushing her teeth and walked back to her room. She got dressed quickly and ran down the stairs.

Maggie turned at the sound of Ginnie coming into the kitchen. "Well, you're sure perky at 6:30 in the morning. Most children your age would be still sleeping in during these summer months."

Ginnie moved to the cupboard to get bowls for the cereal that Maggie had placed on the table and some glasses for the orange juice. "Most *children* don't have a mystery to solve, or should I say a lost Island to find. Although, I don't think I like being classified as a *child.*"

Maggie joined Ginnie at the table and poured corn flakes into her bowl.

"Oh, do forgive me. I had forgotten that you do have the demeanor of someone well beyond her twelve years. But, dear, to someone my age, you're still a child. I have calluses on my foot older than you."

Ginnie almost snorted milk through her nose from laughing at what Maggie said. She really liked her and was glad to have been able to spend this time with her these past few days. She felt bad though about the circumstances that made it come about. This sobering thought reminded her of Aunt Vera.

"Maggie, do you know when Aunt Vera is supposed to be getting out of the hospital? We should probably go and see her again today."

Maggie added some strawberries from a bowl she had placed on the table onto her cornflakes. "I called the hospital last night before going to bed and talked to the nurse on duty. I didn't think I'd be taking her away from too many duties. I mean it is such a small hospital and they only have a few patients at a time, the more serious cases being transferred to the Mainland and..." Maggie paused as she noticed Ginnie rolling her eyes.

"Okay, I know, rambling right? A bad habit that librarians acquire after many years of working in a place where you have to be quiet. Well, what I was about to say is that your Aunt Vera will be coming home this afternoon some time, so we will have time to go and start our research at the library this morning."

As the last spoonful of cereal found its way from Ginnie's mouth and into her stomach, Maggie was already starting to clear away the dishes. "We'll just put them in the sink and head over to the library awhile. You can come with me now and we should have about an hour to ourselves before I have to open the doors to the public. I can at least get you set up at a table with some of the maps awhile and then join you now and then when there's no one that needs my assistance in the library. It doesn't usually get too busy this time of year. Though it does look a bit overcast today. Sometimes the rain brings out the reader in a lot of people."

Ginnie walked with Maggie to the little village that had grown on this island in the past thirty years. She wondered what it had looked like before all the buildings went up and the roads were formed and paved over for smoother riding. There weren't a lot of cars. Most of the people either walked or, if it was a longer jaunt, used a bicycle. They also had a taxi cab that drove people around the island. Maggie told her that it was run by a man named Charlie Burke who retired here a few years ago and got bored so he started up his own cab service.

A sign that had the name of 'PERDU' printed on it stood on the outskirts of the town. Population 200 was printed under the name. Ginnie walked down the main street with Maggie as store owners were readying their shops for business that day.

She had never been down here this early in the day before. It looked as if the town was waking up as vendors unrolled their awnings and grocers carried out fruits and vegetables in huge baskets outside the front of their shops. An old man stood by one of the shops as he watched the owner bringing out buckets of fresh flowers. They were of such bright and beautiful colors that she was sure they were chosen to entice people into his shop. It worked. Ginnie looked longingly at the pretty roses as their sweet scent filled her nostrils.

The old man smiled at her as he lifted a pink rose from one of the deep buckets and gave the owner a dollar. He carefully handed it to her so that she would not be pricked by one of the thorns, tipped his hat to her and turned and walked away. He was gone before she could even say thank you.

"Maggie, did you see that man?"

Maggie was fishing through her purse for her library keys. "I'm sorry dear, what did you say?"

Ginnie showed her the flower that the old man had just given her. "There was an old man standing here and he smiled at me like he knew who I was and bought me this rose. Didn't you see him?"

"I was looking in my purse, so I didn't see him. Where is he now?"

Ginnie looked all around on the street but couldn't see him anywhere.

"He's gone now. That was so strange."

Maggie looked at the rose and shrugged. "He probably has a granddaughter close to your age that you reminded him of and thought it would be a nice gesture. We'll put it in some water when we get to the library."

When they arrived at the library, they still had a little over an hour left before Maggie would have to open for the day. She found an old vase for Ginnie's rose and left it on the check out desk while they moved toward a table in the archives room.

"Not many people come back here unless it's during the school year and they're doing research for a term paper. You should have plenty of privacy. Put your notebook and things down awhile and we can go look for the maps."

Ginnie put down the things she brought with her for her research project. Her notebook that she had used the paper from for her letters, a couple of pencils and the letters from Vicky. She followed Maggie out to the main part of the library where there was a large table with a glass top and wide, shallow drawers. Under the glass on top was a large map of the island and the coast of Nova Scotia in the background. Maggie pulled open some of the drawers until she found the maps she was looking for and would hand them one by one to Ginnie.

"Okay, that should do for now. This first map I gave you should be a copy of one that was printed in the 1890's for this area. This one is for the same era but it shows more because it includes Europe and since they sailed from England, you could try and follow the route they would have taken to get to New York. And this one here that I'm holding is a current map of the same, except of course that's it's been updated to present day."

They carried the maps to the back room and laid them open on the table. It was large enough to hold all the maps as they lay spread out. Maggie perused them with her for a few minutes before looking at her watch.

"I'm going to have to go up front and open the doors in a few minutes. Is there anything else you'll need before I leave you alone to your map reading?"

Ginnie was studying one of the older maps and shook her head as Maggie moved to the door. "Oh, I know. Could I look at that album of newspaper clippings too? There might be something I missed before that I wasn't looking for until now. That probably doesn't make sense but you know what I mean."

Maggie nodded and smiled as she left and returned with the album. "It all makes perfectly sense to me. But of course, I read H.G. Wells."

Maggie closed the door as she left the room and Ginnie sat down and got to work. She traced different routes from England to New York with her finger on the map, considering different possibilities. They were supposed to have been a month at sea already before the storm hit and blew them off course. They should have been pretty close already to their destination. She compared both maps, looking back and forth from one to the other until she was cross eyed and had to take a break.

While rubbing her eyes, she heard the door open and looked up expecting Maggie, since it was nearing lunch time. Aunt Vera was standing in the doorway scowling at her. Ginnie stood up and walked over to where she was still standing by the door. She tried to covertly look over Aunt Vera's shoulder to see if Maggie was close by. Not that she was scared of Aunt Vera, but Maggie seemed to have a calming influence on her.

"She's next door."

Ginnie was confused by Aunt Vera's words. "Who's next door?"

Aunt Vera stepped into the room and shut the door behind her. She took off her sweater and placed it over the back of a chair and laid her purse on the floor.

"Don't be a ninny. I know you were looking for back up. Maggie went next door to get some sandwiches for our lunch. There's no one in the library right now but you and I."

Ginnie didn't know if this was good news or not. If there were other people in the library, maybe her aunt wouldn't yell at her. But then again, with Aunt Vera, you never know if that would stop her anyway. Aunt Vera sighed and then moved over to the table to look at the maps.

"Don't worry. I'm not going to bite your head off. I've been talking to Maggie and doing some thinking in the hospital these past few days, and I realize that I've probably been a little harsh on you this summer, and though it's hard for me to apologize to anyone, I guess if I'm going to ever start, now is a good time."

Ginnie had been walking backwards toward the table as she listened to Aunt Vera talk. As she heard these last words, she fell back onto a handy chair, which was preferable over the cold hard floor. Aunt Vera smiled and Ginnie could've sworn she heard a chuckle come out of her Aunt's mouth.

"How did you know I'd be here at the library?"

"Well, besides the fact that you have been staying for the past couple of days with the town librarian, it wasn't too difficult to figure out. Charlie Burke picked me up at the hospital in his cab and told me he'd seen the two of you walking this way this morning while he was driving around so I had him drop me off here. So, get me up to speed on what you've found out so far. Maggie told me about the second note in the bottle. Can I see it?"

Ginnie, still sitting in the chair that she plopped onto, slid closer to the table and picked up the two pieces of paper that had come from the bottle.

"This is the first one that you've read already and here is the second one."

Aunt Vera took the papers from her hand and read them both before laying them back down on the table. She looked over at the maps that Ginnie and Maggie had laid out on the table.

"Hmmm, so what have you been doing so far.?"

"You mean you don't think its nonsense?"

Vera smiled at Ginnie, and then, to her surprise, winked at her.

"I think I could use a little nonsense in my life right now."

Ginnie jumped up from the chair and moved the maps closer to Aunt Vera. She stood beside her chair as she leaned over and showed the routes she had traced with her finger from London to New York.

"I think this would have been the route they would have taken. It's pretty much the most direct."

Aunt Vera leaned over and looked the map over. She saw where Ginnie was pointing on the older map and compared it to the current one next to it.

"It looks like they could've gotten blown off course right around the Grand Banks by Newfoundland. The storm could've pushed their ship toward Nova Scotia right about here." Aunt Vera pointed to a spot on the map that was marked Halifax. "It wasn't too far from here that the crew was found. My father took me to the spot once after my grandfather had disappeared."

Ginnie noticed that Aunt Vera's voice quivered a little bit when she talked of her father. She put a hand on her shoulder and continued to survey the map with her, as they looked to find any islands that may not have been founded yet in 1892. As they worked together, a sort of unspoken peace developed between them and they were even laughing together when Maggie walked in a few minutes later carrying sandwiches and sodas.

"I'm glad to see you two getting along so well, but let me in on the joke."

Ginnie was holding the second note she had gotten from Vicky and turned it toward Maggie.

"I know it's not funny that they're stuck on this island, but we thought it was amusing that one of the things she writes is that she's running out of stories to tell her little brother."

The three of them sat and ate the sandwiches, tossing back and forth ideas and then discarding them. After Ginnie finished, she asked Maggie to slide the album over to her. She hadn't opened it yet since Maggie left it for her that morning, being so preoccupied with the maps.

Reading through all the articles she came across one of them about the Captain and looked it over again. Maggie chatted a bit with Aunt Vera as they finished their lunch, peeking out into the library every so often to see if anyone was out there. So far it was very quiet. Ginnie got their attention when she stood up and leaned over the old map again.

"According to this article, the Captain said that they were about here before the storm hit. So we were right about the route they took. Is there some way we could find out what the wind speed was during that storm and maybe the ocean currents so that we could plot the course the storm would have driven them?"

Aunt Vera thought for a minute and then asked Maggie for a phone directory.

"We could call the coast guard office on the mainland and see if they keep any kind of records like that. The most they can say is no."

Ginnie tried to keep a rein on the excitement she was feeling. One way or another, between the three of them, they were going to bring Vicky and the Wellesley home.

CHAPTER SEVEN
July 14, 1892

It had been two days since Vicky released the bottle into the ocean. She didn't really think she would get an answer this quickly, or whether she'd get one back at all. Deep inside her, something made her believe that she would. She checked the beach and the pool before helping her family and the others move camp to a small cave that they found in the middle of the island. She hated being away from the shore, but the men thought it would be the safest place if the storm that was brewing was anything like the last one.

There wasn't much room in the dank space so they couldn't build a fire. They had candles from the ship that they lit and placed along crevices on the wall, taking care that none of the children got burned. A lot of them were already asleep for the night including her little brother. Vicky felt an energy in the air. Whether it was from the storm or just the feeling that something was about to happen that would save them, she wasn't sure. It could've been a combination of both.

She looked down at the dress she was wearing. They couldn't bring much with them in the row boat, so she had only two dresses with her that she alternated wearing from day to day. They were both getting pretty grubby by now. The hems were all tattered from walking through the bushes and around the trees, when she had helped gather wood. She looked forward to the day that she could take a nice hot bath that didn't use water that hurt your skin because of the salt in it. Then she would put on a soft and clean cotton night gown and sleep on a soft mattress with fluffy pillows. Her father tugged her braid, pulling her out of her reverie.

"Where were you just now? I know you weren't here in this cave with all these people with a smile like that on your face. You must have been daydreaming, or since its night, I guess it should be night dreaming. Actually, that is what you should be doing right now. The other children have been asleep for hours."

Vicky looked over at the side of the cave where all the children lay asleep huddled together on the blankets and then looked up at her father.

"Do you really expect me to sleep and have sweet dreams crowded in with the others? It would be more like nightmares. I was just thinking about how lovely it would be to have a hot bath and a soft nightgown and a comfortable bed to sleep in all to my own. I'm sorry Papa. I just can't sleep right now. I feel something in the air. Maybe it's the storm that's coming or something else. I don't know. Please let me stay up for a little while longer."

Her father nodded. He understood what she was feeling. He was feeling it too.

"How about we sit up together for awhile? Would you like that?" At her nod, he put his arm around his daughter and hugged her close. "Now tell me more about those lovely things you were dreaming about."

It was a couple of hours later when Vicky opened her eyes. She was still leaning next to her father who was sound asleep. She looked around the cave, and saw that everyone was sleeping somewhere along the floor or leaning against the cave walls. She figured that it must be very late into the night. She stood up carefully so as not to wake her father. She could see the moon peeking through the cloud filled sky outside. It looked like there was a break in the weather. The rain fell silently as it hit the ground. She could hear the sound of thunder but it sounded far away.

She decided that there was enough light for her to find her way to the beach. She turned around once again and saw that no one stirred. Quietly, she tip toed out and followed the path that led to the shore. She was going to check one more time to see if the bottle was there.

She was almost to the beach, when suddenly a bright light shone above her. Then a loud boom roared in her ears. The lightning flashed again and the rain started to beat down harder. The wind started to pick up and tore at her dress. She was too close to turn back now. Just a little farther and then she'd hurry back to the cave.

CHAPTER EIGHT
July 14, 1965

Aunt Vera hung up the phone after talking to the Coast Guard. They were all three sitting in Aunt Vera's kitchen where they spread the maps on her kitchen table.

"They said it would take a lot of research to get the wind velocity for that storm. It was one that had not been predicted so that no one knew it was coming. The currents they were able to help us with. It seems they keep records of the tides and did have what they would have been at that time. Though without knowing which direction or what speed the winds were blowing, it may not be of much help."

Maggie got up and picked up the tea kettle off the stove and filled it with water from the tap.

"I think we all need a tea break. Vera, do you have anything sweet like cookies or cake to eat in your kitchen? I think we could use something right now."

Vera picked up a cookie canister from her counter and brought it over to the table. She grabbed some plates and cups from the cupboard and set them around for everyone.

"How about some chocolate chip cookies?"

Ginnie and Maggie smiled at each other. Maggie poured the hot water over the teabags in the teapot and placed it on the table.

"I guess that'll have to do."

Aunt Vera invited Maggie to stay for dinner, and afterward Ginnie was going to walk home with her and pick up the clothes and toothbrush she had left at her house. They all pitched in together with the making of the meal. Maggie started the roast. Ginnie peeled potatoes and covered them with water and placed them on the stove. Aunt Vera shucked some peas and placed them on the stove to simmer.

Maggie and Ginnie made sure that Aunt Vera had all her medicines and that she had taken her blood pressure pills. At first, Aunt Vera scowled at them for fussing over her. Her face softened though, knowing that they cared about her to make sure she didn't get sick. She knew she was going to miss Ginnie when she went back home at the end of the summer.

As they were finishing up their meal, Aunt Vera glanced out the kitchen window.

"If you're going to walk Maggie home, Ginnie, the two of you might want to get a move on pretty soon. It looks as black as night out there and it's only six o'clock."

Ginnie and Maggie both stood up and stood in front of the window. Light rain pellets began to hit the window.

"It looks like it's going to be another one of those storms like you had a few weeks ago when all that debris washed up on the beach. I remember because right after that is when I found that bottle…."

Ginnie caught her breath and just froze still for a second. Maggie and Aunt Vera turned and looked at her wondering if she was okay.

"Are you okay, Ginnie? Maybe you should wait until tomorrow to pick up your stuff from Maggie's. You don't look too well."

Ginnie turned away from the window and looked back and forth at the both of them and then said one word.

"Map."

Maggie looked at Aunt Vera and then shrugged. Both of them stared at Ginnie, hoping that she would eventually make sense.

Ginnie started running around the kitchen moving things on the counter. She looked around the room frantically searching for something.

Maggie couldn't stand it anymore.

"Ginnie what are you looking for?"

Ginnie stood still in the middle of the kitchen and looked at them as if they were supposed to understand what she was talking about.

"Map…Where did you put the maps that we were looking at?"

Aunt Vera went into the living room and came back into the kitchen holding the three maps they had been looking at earlier.

"If this was what you were looking for, why didn't you just say so? You know we moved them off the table so we could eat dinner."

Ginnie moved to the table and started clearing the plates off and putting them in the sink. She took the maps from Aunt Vera and unfolded them across the table.

"I think I've just figured out where Vicky and the passengers of the Wellesley are stranded."

Aunt Vera and Maggie both gasped and hurried over to stand beside Ginnie at the table. Aunt Vera was the first to find her voice, never having been a problem for her before.

"How did you figure it out? We couldn't find anything on the maps and we studied them all afternoon."

Ginnie picked up her notebook that she had placed on the counter earlier and pulled out the two notes from Vicky that she had tucked inside.

"The first note didn't mention any date so I didn't think too much about it, but I remember that the second note did."

She unfolded both notes, finding the one she was looking for.

"See, on this one she writes that it is the twelfth of July. I found this one on the twelfth of July. But it was July 12, 1965 and she's writing this on July 12, 1892. We are living the same day and the same month, but seventy-three years apart. Aunt Vera, you said that the worst storm was right before I came out here for the summer, in May. Do you remember exactly when in May it was?"

Aunt Vera thought for a minute then looked at Maggie.

"Wasn't it around the end of May, Maggie?"

Maggie mulled it over for a minute then nodded.

"Yes, I remember now because I had to close the library early that day. The storm hit so hard it almost blew me over while I made my way home. It was on the 26th."

Ginnie looked at the notes she had made from the newspaper clippings in her notebook.

"The Captain of the Wellesley said that the storm hit on the 26th of May of 1892."

She let Aunt Vera and Maggie absorb that for awhile. Letting them figure out for themselves what she already had a few minutes before. She saw the light go on when both their mouths suddenly fell open.

"Yes, you see it don't you? When the storm hit this island in May of 1965, it also hit the Wellesley in May of 1892 because the Wellesley was here. The island they're stranded on is this one, but seventy-three years ago. Look at the map. The reason that the only island we could find that didn't show up on the older map was Perdu is because this is the island."

Maggie and Vera sat down and stared at the map. It made sense, in a non-sensical sort of way. Looking at all the pieces in a different way now, it all fit together like a finished jig saw puzzle.

Ginnie sat down too and grabbed her notebook. Tearing out a piece of paper she grabbed a pencil and looked at the two women for inspiration on what to write to Vicky.

"I need to send another letter in the bottle and send it to her tonight. The reason the bottle kept finding its way back and forth with our letters is because it never left the island, just the century, which in my opinion is a much farther trip.

What should I tell her? Will telling them where they are help them get back? There has to be something more to it than that."

Maggie got up and filled the tea pot and set it to boil.

"I need another cup of tea before thinking this through. I'm not in any hurry getting home tonight the way it looks out there right now."

Aunt Vera got up and opened her refrigerator.

"The heck with tea, I need something stronger." She frowned when she didn't find what she was looking for. "Where's that tin of coffee I had in here?"

Maggie set two cups on the counter and poured them each a cup of tea.

"I threw it away while you were in the hospital. Your doctor told me that you're not supposed to have so much coffee when you're taking pills for your blood pressure. Sit down and I'll fix you a cup of tea and I'll make it extra strong for you."

Ginnie couldn't sit still much longer.

"Ladies, can we please get back to saving a lot of people who are stranded on this island in this same storm but with probably a lot less shelter than we have over our heads right now?"

Aunt Vera reluctantly took the cup of tea that Maggie poured for her and sat back down at the table.

"Hmmph, the impudence of some people."

Maggie, carrying her own cup of tea, joined them at the table once again.

"She's not being impudent, Vera. She's right you know, we do have to figure this out."

Vera looked over at Maggie and scowled.

"I wasn't talking about Ginnie. I was talking about you."

Maggie ignored Vera and mulled over all the facts they had in front of them.

"It's got to be something about the storms that hit that is causing all this to happen. How else could you explain the crew winding up on one shore and the passengers along with the ship on another. The weirdest thing about it is the crew. At least the passengers have been aware all this time and remember what happened to them. But the crew wake up from some comatose state and it's almost two months later."

Ginnie started doodling on the piece of paper while she listened. She drew swirling lines around and around on the paper until she finally realized what she was doing and stopped. Aunt Vera and Maggie stopped talking when they realized that Ginnie was not saying anything. They looked over to see her staring at the drawing she made.

"Aunt Vera, Maggie, I think I might have figured it out. I remember my dad talking to someone once about quantum theories dealing with time travel and some other stuff I don't remember because it was way above my head for me to understand. But I do remember something he said about there sometimes can be an opening, sort of like a portal. Maggie you should probably dig this because of that H.G. Wells guy and his time machine."

Maggie looked pleased that she remembered the author's name.

"Well, anyway, what I'm thinking is that the Wellesley got caught in the vortex or the very center of the storm. Look at my drawing. See all the swirling lines. That's the storm and the very center of it is where the ship happened to be at the wrong time. Time being the key word here. Maggie, do you think it's possible that the storm was so fierce that it created an opening for a time portal?"

Maggie looked at Ginnie's drawing and then thought for a minute.

"You know, that could be the reason the crew got separated from the ship. Here they are fighting this storm and then suddenly all is calm. They always say that in the eye of a storm it's completely calm. They reach the vortex and the Captain and the crew, who are on top, enter this portal and are probably only in it a few minutes but when they come out, time has passed much quicker and almost two months have gone by. That's why they can't remember the past two months, because to them it had only been two minutes and they had blacked out during most of that."

Aunt Vera remembered what her grandfather and the rest of the crew had to face when they were found. No one would have believed any of this back then. But she believed it now.

"Maggie, I think you're right. The passengers were at the lower part of the ship and weren't swept into the vortex like the crew. They were stranded and were so scared after finding the Captain and the crew missing, that all they could think of was to row to the nearest island and wait for help. They must have got tired of waiting though, because no trace of them was ever found when this island was discovered. I wonder if they finally decided to board the ship once again and try to sail it but never made it."

Ginnie thought about that but decided against it.

"I don't think so because some trace of them should have been found by now. They wouldn't have had to go very far to find help. Look how close they would've been to the mainland? I think they got caught up in a place suspended in time. The Captain and the crew were sort of thrown from the portal, but the passengers and the ship remained in it all these years. There must be a way that they can sail the ship through this storm tonight and close the portal behind them. This is about the same time seventy-three years ago that the Captain and the crew were found. I think they need to do it tonight or they may never get another chance."

CHAPTER NINE
July 14, 1892

Vicky could barely see anything when she finally made it to the pool. She searched around the edge between the plants until her hand brushed against something hard. It was the bottle. She grabbed it and didn't bother opening it. She would do that once she returned to the shelter. The wind was making it difficult to move and she kept falling down in the sand. This last time there was a hand reaching out to her to help her up. As she brushed the wet hair from her face, she could see her papa standing over her.

"Victoria, what are you doing out here? How dare you leave the cave and venture out here alone?"

He did not wait for a response, but picked her up and carried her back to where the others were sleeping. Once inside he put her down and wrapped a blanket around her.

"You're going to have to get out of those wet things before you catch pneumonia. What were you thinking about going out there like that?"

Her mother was awake when they had returned and was already getting some dry clothes out for her. Her father held a blanket up while her mother helped her change. Some of the other people woke up when they heard them moving around. Vicky held up the bottle for her father to see.

"Papa, I found the bottle. I just knew it would be there. Look, there's another letter inside. Please yell at me later, but open the bottle now."

She handed it over to her father and let him open it this time. He still frowned as he stared at the bottle and then pulled out the cork. He turned the bottle over in his hand and pulled out the note. His frown changed to an expression of shock as he read the note.

Dear Vicky,

We have figured out where you are and can give you directions home. However you must do it tonight or you may never make it. This may be hard to believe, but you are stranded on the same island that I'm living on right now with my Aunt Vera. The only difference is that it is 1892 where you are and 1965 where I am right now. Our days coincide because it is the evening of July 14 for us and I believe it is the same for you. If I am correct, you have a pretty good storm brewing and probably won't think its good sailing weather but that's exactly what you have to do. It was the storm that brought you there and it is the storm that will take you home. Please believe me. You are on an island that's just across from Nova Scotia and you don't have too far to go to get to safety but you must do it now.

Your Friend through all time,

Ginnie Maitlin

"What does the letter say, Papa?"

Jacob Trenton reread the note three times before handing it to Vicky. Her mother looked over her shoulder as they read it together. They both looked up at him when they finished. They could hear some of the other men stirring behind them. One of them had noticed the bottle and asked if another letter had come in it. When he saw what Vicky was holding, he asked to read it. Vicky's father nodded to her to hand it to him.

"This is crazy. None of us are experienced sailors. It would be hard enough for us to steer that ship in calm weather yet alone that raging tempest out there!"

The man's voice rose louder as he spoke, waking more of the others. Soon they were surrounded by most of the other passengers except for the children who still slept. Jacob passed the note around so that everyone had a chance to read it.

"We have a decision to make and we need to make it now. I know what's written in that letter sounds crazy but has anything felt sane since this whole thing started? I know if we try and sail the ship we'll be risking our lives and the lives of our children. I myself have my wife Moira and my daughter Vicky and son John to think about. I think I am thinking about them in taking this risk. But we either all go or we all stay, no one will be left behind. I think I speak for my family when I say we are willing to take the risk."

He was about to turn away to let them talk when one of the women stepped forward.

"I'm willing to take the risk." No sooner had she finished saying this than a man behind her started sputtering as his face turned red with rage.

"Miranda you come back here right now. No one asked for your opinion."

She ignored her husband and stood her ground. Another woman stepped forward.

"I'm willing to take the risk too."

Then another woman, followed by several more, all stated that they were willing to take the risk along with their children. The husbands were shocked into silence and soon relented. They were afraid their wives would convince Jacob Trenton to leave them behind.

The next few minutes passed in a flurry as they packed up their belongings and woke the children to get them ready for the trek to the ship. Jacob advised some of the men to lead in the front and the rest follow in the rear so that they could make sure no child wandered off. He asked the women to hold onto the children while the men carried their belongings and when everyone was ready, led them out of the cave.

The journey to the beach was tiring as the wind pushed them back relentlessly. The rain soaked them through within minutes and the children were frightened by the thunder and lightning. After much effort though, they finally made it to the shore. That was the easy part.

Untying the boats took some time. They had tied them securely to the trees and the knots were wet and hard to undo. When they finally got them untied, they loaded everyone in them and started rowing out to the ship. The water was choppy and it took them a long time to row out to the ship, and when they finally made it many a face wore a funny shade of green.

The rowboats swayed in the choppy water while everyone tried to get on board. A few of the men climbed up on the rope ladder, slippery from the rain, with great difficulty. Once they got to the top, they helped the women climb up. The men in the rowboats lifted the children as high as they could reach for the men in the Wellesley to grab.

They left the life boats behind in the water rather than even bothering to try to secure them to the ship. They had enough to deal with as it was. The men asked the women to go below deck with the children for safety.

The women decided to listen to their husbands and did as they were told. They followed the stairs down that led to the hold below and went to the cabins they had occupied before they were stranded on the island.

Vicky watched her mother place her little brother on the bed and then turn to her.

"Come on honey, you lie down next to your little brother. It's going to get rough."

Vicky shook her head no and helped her mother tuck her brother in.

"I was okay the first time we came through this storm, I'll be okay again, Mama."

Her mother looked as if she was about to argue with her and then changed her mind and smiled.

"Let's at least stay close together with Johnny on the bed so we can hold onto each other if it does start to get really choppy."

Vicky nodded and joined her mother on the bed, remembering not too long ago being down here waiting while her father was up on deck in the midst of the storm.

The men who had some sailing knowledge were put in charge of securing the sails and the rigging. Jacob had assisted the Helmsman with the wheel during the storm so he took over the wheel. Each man had a job to do to get the ship on its way. The storm was hitting them hard now and Jacob fought hard to keep control of the Wellesley.

He turned the ship and headed directly into the storm. Everyone was too busy fighting the wind to be afraid. The streaming rain made it hard to see, but still they held steadfast to their course, the ship tossing to and fro in the roiling waves.

At one point, Jacob was afraid they were going down when the ship plunged forward and then rolled backward, almost overturning into the sea. At that point he had lost his grip on the wheel. He struggled to get control back and right the ship once again.

No one kept track of time while they fought the storm, so no one really knew how long it was before suddenly everything was calm again. There was silence all around them and the ocean was completely still.

Jacob was able to let go of the wheel. It didn't move an inch. His hands were sore from the tight grip he used to hold a steady course. The day looked strange. There was no darkness to indicate night or light to indicate day. Looking at the sky didn't help either. It was a silvery shade of gray. Suddenly everything went black and Jacob and the other men on deck lost consciousness.

Jacob Trenton opened his eyes and stared at the blue sky above him. Seagulls were flying over the ship and he could hear the sea breezes ruffling the sails. He sat up slowly and saw the other men do the same. They were not alone.

The Captain and the crew of the Wellesley were once again on board the ship.

CHAPTER TEN
July 15, 1965

It was a little after midnight and Ginnie, Aunt Vera, and Maggie, who decided to stay the night, sat around the kitchen table. They could still hear the winds howling outside and the rain hitting the roof with intensity.

Ginnie had returned a little while ago from delivering her message in the bottle for she believed would be the last time. She was soaking wet when she entered the house and Aunt Vera made her run upstairs and take off her clothes and put on some dry pajamas.

"I feel like we're waiting for something to happen. I mean, I left the message for Vicky and the others to find and if they do and decide to believe it and sail the ship in this storm, it's going to change a lot of things isn't it?"

Aunt Vera looked at her thoughtfully.

"What do you mean dear?"

Maggie was at the stove stirring something in a small pot.

"I know what she means, Vera. When something happened one way in history and then you change it, it could cause a chain reaction of other changes. You know, like if someone had originally died young but that has changed so that they live a longer life, get married and have children that normally wouldn't have been born."

Ginnie nodded which caused a wet strand of hair to fall over her face that she brushed aside with her hand.

"That's it exactly. I've been sitting here watching the storm and knowing that at this very moment they're probably either sailing through it or getting ready to, that's if Vicky was able to convince them, and waiting for something to change. How is it going to affect this island or even the world, when all these people that supposedly were never found, come back to civilization and continue to live a full life? The children will grow up and maybe become president or some important person who could make an important decision that could affect a lot of people."

Maggie grabbed some cups from the cupboard.

"Well, I don't think any drastic changes are going to happen in this kitchen in the next few minutes so let's all have some warm milk."

Ginnie wrinkled her nose at the thought of drinking warm milk.

"Put a little cocoa in mine and I'll have some."

Maggie went to the pantry to find the cocoa.

"That sounds like a good idea. I'll make them all cocoa."

Aunt Vera harrumphed. "There, a change in this kitchen has already occurred. For once she's not making tea."

CHAPTER ELEVEN
July 15, 1965

Everything was quiet when Maggie opened her eyes. She and Maggie and Aunt Vera finished their hot cocoas and then decided to go to bed and await whatever may happen while tucked comfortably among the covers. It took a long time for Ginnie to finally fall asleep but then she slept soundly until just now when the sunlight streaking in her room awakened her.

Something didn't look right. There were no rosebuds on the wall paper that were normally there in the room she slept in at Aunt Vera's. She sat up in her bed and looked around, realizing suddenly what was different. This wasn't the room at Aunt Vera's house. This was her own bedroom in her parent's house in Washington D.C. How did she get here?

She rose from the bed and looked around. Everything was like it usually was in her room. Her parents were in Europe. This didn't make any sense. She walked over to her door and opened it and stood in the hallway listening for any signs of movement.

She could hear someone in the kitchen and walked down the stairs and stood in the doorway to see who it was. Her mother was making toast, while her father was sitting at the table drinking coffee and reading the paper. She rushed into the room.

"What are you guys doing here? You're supposed to be in Europe."

Her mother took the toast out of the toaster and turned to look at her while her father lowered his newspaper.

"What are you talking about Virginia? We're not scheduled to leave for another week. Your mother and I had planned on leaving earlier, but some of the British diplomats were going to be here in the states this week and they decided to hold a special dinner for them at the Embassy. You already know all this, you've been invited to go."

Ginnie's mouth fell open.

"I've been invited to go to Europe?"

Her mother smiled as she placed more bread in the toaster for Ginnie.

"No, silly, you've been invited to the dinner. For some reason, someone at the British Embassy wanted to meet you. It's very unusual for a child to be invited. But we've already talked about this. Are you feeling okay?"

Ginnie poured herself a glass of milk and sat down at the table where her mother placed a plate of toast for her.

"Yeah, I'm okay. I guess I'm just not fully awake yet. I feel like I'm still dreaming."

That afternoon, Ginnie and her mother went shopping for new dresses. Ginnie was still feeling strange about waking up in Washington when she went to bed in Perdu. She hoped that it would all explain itself eventually. She would really like to talk to Aunt Vera and Maggie. But for now, she was going to enjoy this shopping moment with her mother.

She hadn't realized how much she had missed her parents while they had been in Europe. It was going to be worse this time because she'll only have them back for a week before they leave all over again for the trip that they should have already been on and she'll miss them all over again. I wonder if I'm going to be staying with Aunt Vera. She was afraid to ask her parents where she'd be staying while they were gone because she was probably supposed to know already and they would really wonder if something was wrong with her.

That evening, Ginnie put on her new dinner dress. It was light blue and silky and came down to her ankles. Her mother put silver barrettes in her dark hair for her and she almost felt like a princess.

Ginnie and her parents arrived at the Embassy at the same time that a lot of other people were arriving. They were taken to a banquet hall where everyone was seated at a long table that stood in the middle of the room. Long white linen table cloths were draped along the entire table. There were silver candelabras with white candles and bowls of white gardenias placed evenly across the table.

White printed place cards showed the seating arrangement and Ginnie and her parents were seated toward the head of the table.

"Look at this Virginia, they have you next to the head of the table."

She looked over at where her father was pointing and felt nervous. Why would they want her sitting there? It should be her father. Someone must have made a mistake.

"Maybe you should sit there dad and I'll sit between you and mom."

Her father pulled the chair out for her and beckoned her to sit.

"No, honey, it has your name, you sit there."

Ginnie sat and watched the people meander in as they seated themselves along the table. Most of the chairs were filled now except for the one next to her. An old woman dressed in an elegant silver gown completed the party as she took her place next to Ginnie. She wore her gray hair up on the top of her head, while blue sapphires sparkled on her ear lobes. They matched the pendant that hung around her neck.

Brown eyes smiled at Ginnie as the women looked over at where she was sitting. The lady sat at the head of the table, looking so regal that she could have been a member of British royalty. The thought that she could be made Ginnie even more nervous. She leaned over and whispered to her father. "Dad, do you know who this lady is? Is she like the Queen or something?"

The lady chuckled as she overheard this conversation. "No Virginia, I'm not the Queen, though I was named for one."

Ginnie turned her head to look at the women seated next to her. After a few seconds, it finally hit her. "Vicky?!"

Her father, overhearing her remark, scowled at her. "Virginia! You don't address your elders in that fashion! She's Lady Teasdale to you."

Vicky shook her head at Ginnie's father. "That's quite alright. Ginnie and I are friends from way back, aren't we Ginnie? Though I guess that I am very much your elder, by lets see…seventy three years, isn't it?"

Ginnie smiled at her father's shocked face before answering. "Actually, I believe it's only seventy two. I was a year older than you at the time, if you recall."

Vicky and Ginnie were enjoying the confused expression that appeared on her father's face.

"It's okay V—I mean Lady Teasdale. I'll explain it to him later." Ginnie smiled at her dad. She looked back over at Vicky. "It's hard to think of you as Lady Teasdale. So, what happened after you left the island that night?"

Vicky paused as waiters came into the room and placed plates of cheese and crackers in front of the guests. Once left alone again, she leaned in toward Ginnie. "It was a frightening experience. My father, bless his soul, didn't hesitate in his decision of leaving on the ship. But some of the others were skeptical, which I guess is understandable."

Ginnie watched Vicky place some cheese onto her cracker, and followed suit. They both began to nibble, while Vicky continued her story. "Well, some of the women were just as tired of being on the island as we were and stepped forward. Once their husbands realized that they were serious, they had no choice but to go along."

"It was a rough trek to the ship, and once we got aboard didn't get much easier. The women went below decks with the children, and the men did a fantastic job of steering us through the storm."

Vicky nodded at the waiter when he offered her some coffee. The waiter then looked over at Ginnie. "I'll just have water, thank you."

Vicky chuckled as she noticed both of Ginnie's parents listening in to their conversation, a look of shock on both their faces. "After what seemed like hours, there was that quiet again, like there was after the first storm. My mother and I went up on deck shortly after that, along with some of the other women, to find that the Captain and the crew were back on the Wellesley. We stopped at Halifax for supplies, and sailed on until we finally made it to New York. I met Lord Teasdale at a dinner party given by my parents some years later, and moved back to London with him. The rest, as they say, is history."

They were already serving the entrée of roasted pheasant by the time Vicky caught Ginnie up on the last seventy-three years.

Ginnie leaned closer to Vicky. "It looks like my parents are having trouble believing what they're hearing."

Vicky nodded. "I'm not surprised. I lived it and still have trouble believing it. My grandchildren think that it's only a fairy tale that I've made up, along with the other stories I tell them."

"Speaking of which, did you ever run out of stories for your little brother while you were on the island?"

Vicky smiled. "No, thank goodness. I was able to keep him amused with stories about magical bottles."

By the time that they were serving dessert, Vicky had regaled Ginnie with some of the stories she had told her little brother. Ginnie took a bite of strawberry shortcake. After swallowing, she asked, "Whatever happened to Johnny?"

"As it so happens, I will be seeing him this weekend. How would you like to come with me and meet him? Why don't we invite your parents for tea tomorrow afternoon and we'll tell them the whole story."

CHAPTER TWELVE
An Island of the Coast of Nova Scotia—July 22, 1965

Ginnie disembarked from the ferry accompanied by Lady Teasdale, the latter's companion carrying their suitcases. Charlie Burke, the cab driver, was waiting at the dock. He took the bags and put them in the trunk while the others climbed into the cab. They drove through the village, passing the library on the way to Aunt Vera's house.

As they pulled up into the driveway, Ginnie noticed that the house looked different. Where there used to be just a small patch of lawn, there was now a back deck and a pool. The house was larger, too. Ginnie turned to Vicky, a look of bewilderment on her face. "This doesn't look like Aunt Vera's house. The Vera McKuen I stayed with didn't have a swimming pool. The summer would have been a lot less boring with that. Granted, I probably wouldn't have found the bottle then, unless it had washed up in the pool."

Vicky looked up at the house. "This isn't Vera McKuen's house. This is Vera Trenton's house. Vera and John Trenton's house."

Ginnie was stunned. "Your brother and my great aunt are married? When did that happen?"

"Right before John decided to buy this island."

Ginnie looked up at Vicky. "John bought this island? He was the one who was lost in his yacht and found the island? Maggie told me about it when she explained how Perdu got its name. But how could that have been your brother when at the time you all were technically stuck in limbo on this same island? How did he get lost here by himself?"

Vicky chuckled. "Well, he wasn't exactly lost. It was more like returning. John remembered all the stories I told him. A lot of the adventures that I made up came from our life on the island and, of course, the bottle. He was so young when it all happened that years later after he made his money following in our father's footsteps in banking, he decided to visit the island now that its location was known. He was surprised to discover it still deserted and decided to build a house on it and move here. When he saw that other people were interested in coming here from the mainland, he built a school and a hospital too and soon a whole town grew out of one little boy's love for stories."

Anxious to get back to town, Charlie Burke opened the door of the taxi, hoping Ginnie would take the hint. She was just leaning out when Vicky put a hand on her arm.

"One more thing dear that I think you should know. Your Great Aunt Vera and her friend Maggie do not have any recollection of what transpired between us. For some reason, you and I are the only ones who remember. Johnny only knows because of the stories I told him and he always believed them. I think that if we tried to explain it to them, they would find it as hard to comprehend as your parents did when we had tea with them last week. Aunt Vera you've already met before, but you'll have to reintroduce yourself to Maggie. As far as she knows, this is the first time you've been to the island. You'll still find her at the library. That much still hasn't changed."

Ginnie hopped out of the cab and turned to help Vicky out. Miss Thompson, her companion, tipped Charlie to bring the suitcases up to the door. No sooner had he dropped the last one, he was down the steps and back in his cab pulling out of the driveway. Ginnie turned as she heard the front door open.

"Vicky, it's so good to see you again. John is in the kitchen making tea. He always says that I don't make it right. That's an Englishman for you. Always has to have his tea a certain way. Me, personally, I can't stand the stuff. Give me coffee any day."

Ginnie couldn't believe the person standing at the door was Aunt Vera. She was beautiful. Her skin glowed from the sun and her silver hair was cut stylishly short. She wore a turquoise sun dress and sandals. This was not the scowling and pale woman who wore her hair in a bun that she saw last week. Though apparently, she still didn't care for tea.

"You're not supposed to drink coffee, remember?"

Vera looked down at Ginnie and smiled as she hugged her.

"Ginnie, I forgot you were standing there. It's good to see you again. You were so little the last time I saw you and now we get to spend some time together. Your parents should go off to Europe more often. What was that you said about coffee? Why am I not supposed to drink it?"

Ginnie stood back from Aunt Vera's hug. She didn't know if she could get used to the new and improved Vera.

"Too much coffee is not good for you when you're taking high blood pressure medicine."

Aunt Vera raised her eye brows inquiringly at Vicky who merely shrugged in reply.

"I guess that's true, but fortunately, I don't take any. Now come on inside everyone so we can sit down and visit."

Ginnie opened her mouth to dispute Aunt Vera on her medicine when Vicky, anticipating what she was about to do, nudged her. When she looked over at her, Vicky shook her head slightly so no one else noticed and whispered to her.

"She doesn't need those pills. She's been happily married to my brother for many years and living on this island. She doesn't have high blood pressure. Remember, a lot of things changed that only you and I are aware of."

Ginnie nodded and followed them into the house. The inside was just as different as it had been on the outside. The walls were painted white and there were paintings of ocean scenes scattered along the walls. The fire place was a lot bigger, and the furniture a lot newer. She couldn't wait to see what her room looked like. She was sure that there wouldn't be any worn wall paper with faded rose buds on it.

As Ginnie stood in the hall, she noticed something that stood out behind some flowers on the mantle of the fireplace. She moved closer to see what it was. Displayed there was an antique wine bottle. It looked very familiar.

Vicky walked up behind her. "I carried it with me on the voyage back on the Wellesley. John insisted on keeping it, so I relinquished it into his hands for safe keeping."

They all followed Aunt Vera into the kitchen. Ginnie caught a glimpse of the back of John's head as he puttered behind the counter setting up the tea tray. There were all new modern appliances in the kitchen along with flag stone floors. The table was the same antique one she sat at a week ago. She was glad for the one familiar thing in the room. Her head was starting to spin from all the changes she'd seen in the last week.

They all sat down around the table as John came over carrying a tray that held a tea pot, a pitcher of cream, and bowl of sugar. Nestled between the tea things was a plate of scones that looked and smelled like they just came from the oven. Ginnie looked up to thank John and the words caught in her throat. John was the old man who had bought her the rose. He winked at her as he offered her a scone. She smiled as she took one and placed it on her plate.

"Thanks Mr. Trenton. They smell good. Almost as good as a rose."

He laid the plate down on the table and smiled back at her.

"You're welcome Ginnie. Sometimes it just feels good to give a beautiful young lady a special treat. And there's no more of this Mr. Trenton, call me John."

"Thank you, John, I mean, Uncle John."

They sat and chatted and laughed and enjoyed the scones. After awhile, Aunt Vera and Uncle John and Vicky went upstairs to rest before supper. Miss Thompson busied herself unpacking Lady Teasdale's belongings.

Ginnie thought this was a great opportunity for her to walk to town and 'meet' the librarian. As she walked pass the town sign, she had to stop and turn around and go back to look at it. It no longer said "Perdu" on it. The sign had changed too.

Welcome to the town of
Perdu et Trouve
(Lost and Found)
Population: 251 and still growing

0-595-33596-9

Printed in the United States
25670LVS00003B/347